Dedicated to Sam, for believing
in a ghost named Simon

Tundra Books, an imprint of Penguin Random House Canada Young Readers,
a division of Penguin Random House of Canada Limited

Library and Archives Canada Cataloguing in Publication

Title: Super detectives / Cale Atkinson.
Names: Atkinson, Cale, author, illustrator.
Description: Series statement: Simon and Chester
Identifiers: Canadiana (print) 20200182447 | Canadiana (ebook) 20200182455
ISBN 9780735267428 (hardcover) | ISBN 9780735267435 (EPUB)
Subjects: LCGFT: Graphic novels.
Classification: LCC PN6733.A85 S87 2021 | DDC j741.5/971—dc23

Published simultaneously in the United States of America by Tundra Books of Northern
New York, an imprint of Penguin Random House Canada Young Readers, a division of
Penguin Random House of Canada Limited

Library of Congress Control Number: 2020933320
Edited by Samantha Swenson
Designed by John Martz
This book was rendered in ectoplasm, pug fur and Photoshop.
The text was set in Silver Age BB.

Printed and bound in China

www.penguinrandomhouse.ca

1   2   3   4   5   25   24   23   22   21

Penguin
Random House
TUNDRA BOOKS

Simon AND Chester

Super Detectives!

by Cale Atkinson

tundra

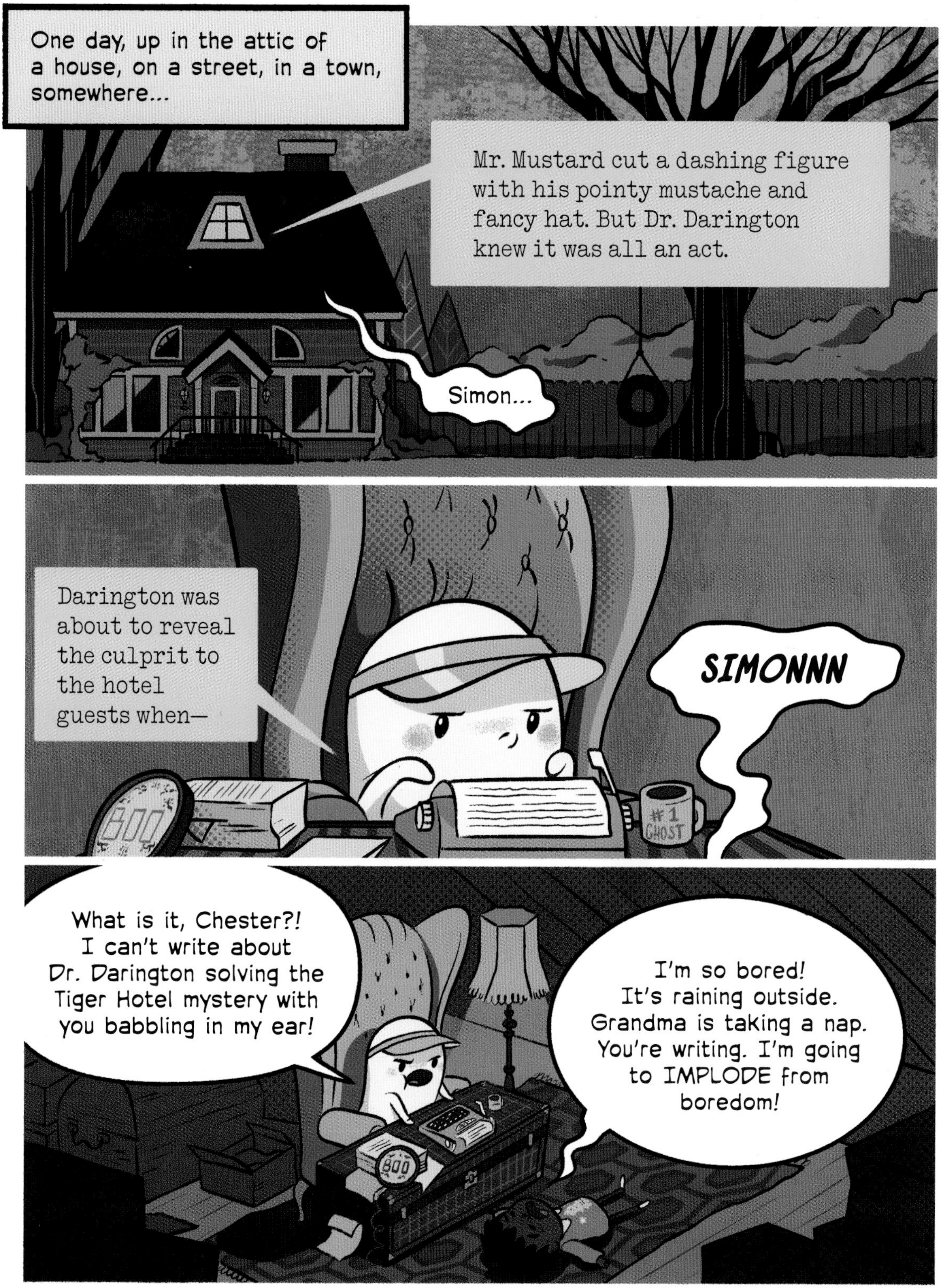
One day, up in the attic of a house, on a street, in a town, somewhere...
Mr. Mustard cut a dashing figure with his pointy mustache and fancy hat. But Dr. Darington knew it was all an act.
Simon...
Darington was about to reveal the culprit to the hotel guests when—
SIMONNN
BOO
#1 GHOST
What is it, Chester?! I can't write about Dr. Darington solving the Tiger Hotel mystery with you babbling in my ear!
I'm so bored! It's raining outside. Grandma is taking a nap. You're writing. I'm going to IMPLODE from boredom!

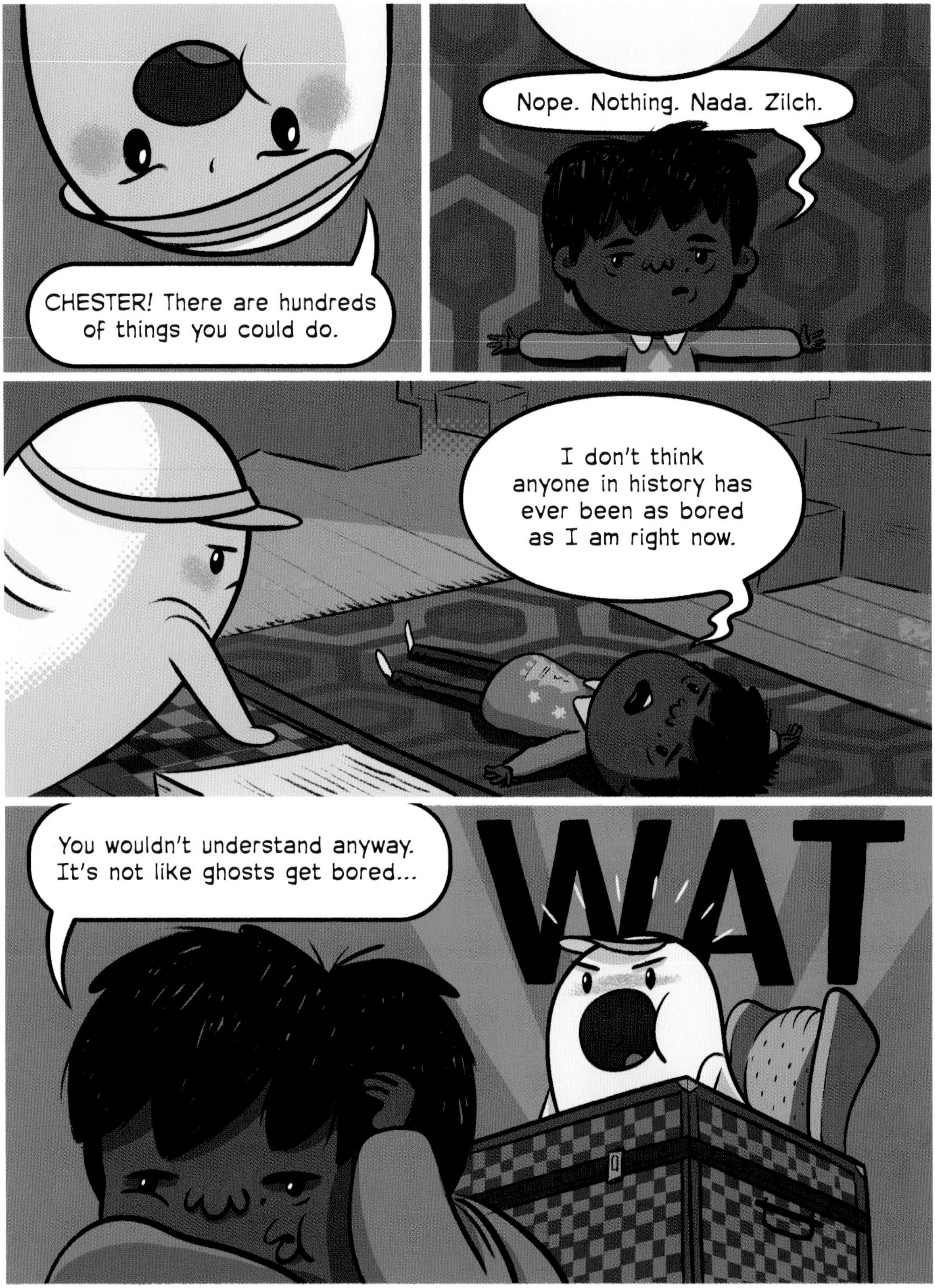
CHESTER! There are hundreds of things you could do.
Nope. Nothing. Nada. Zilch.
I don't think anyone in history has ever been as bored as I am right now.
You wouldn't understand anyway. It's not like ghosts get bored...
WAT

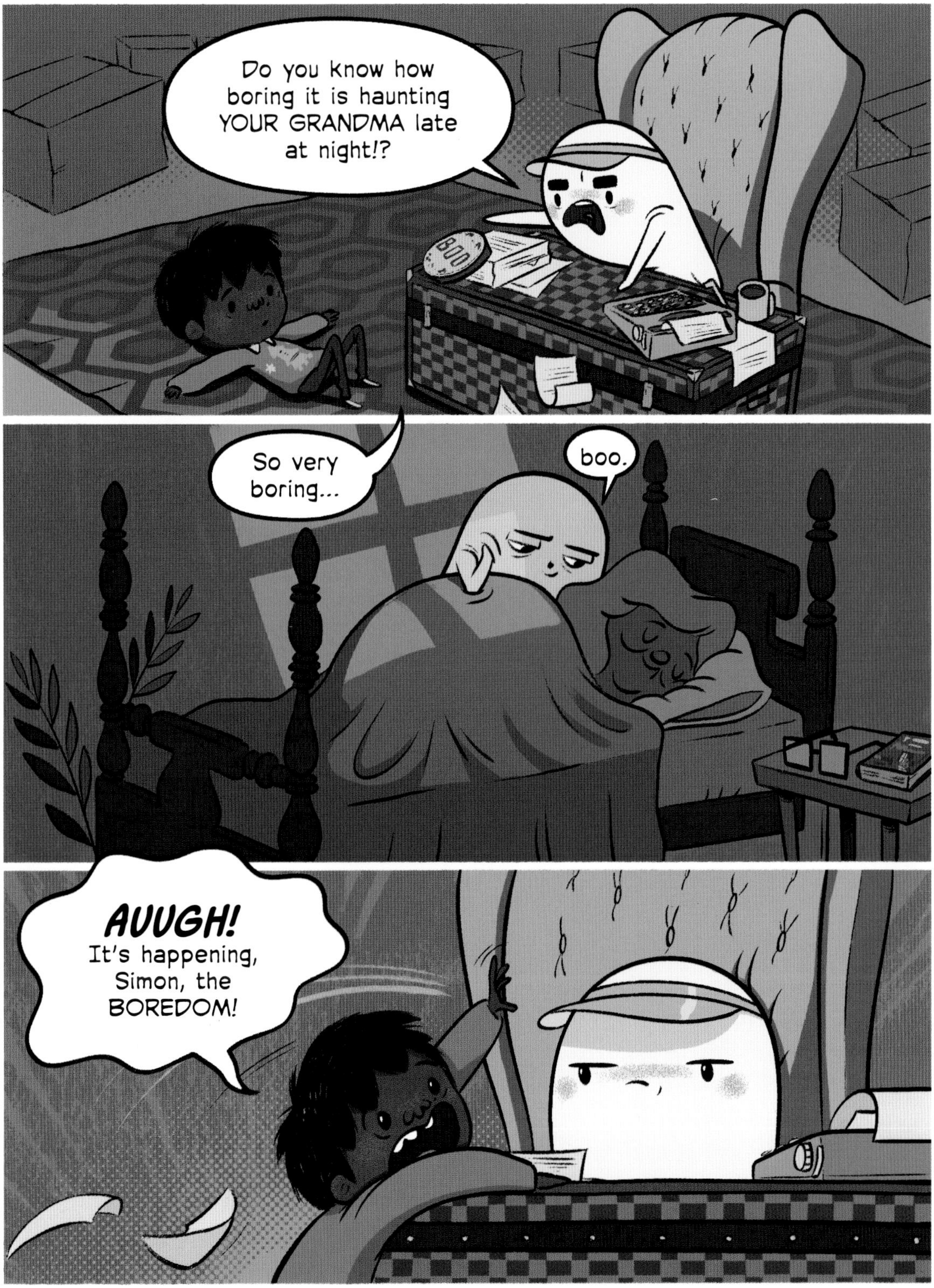
Do you know how boring it is haunting YOUR GRANDMA late at night!?
BOO
So very boring...
boo.
AUUGH!
It's happening, Simon, the BOREDOM!

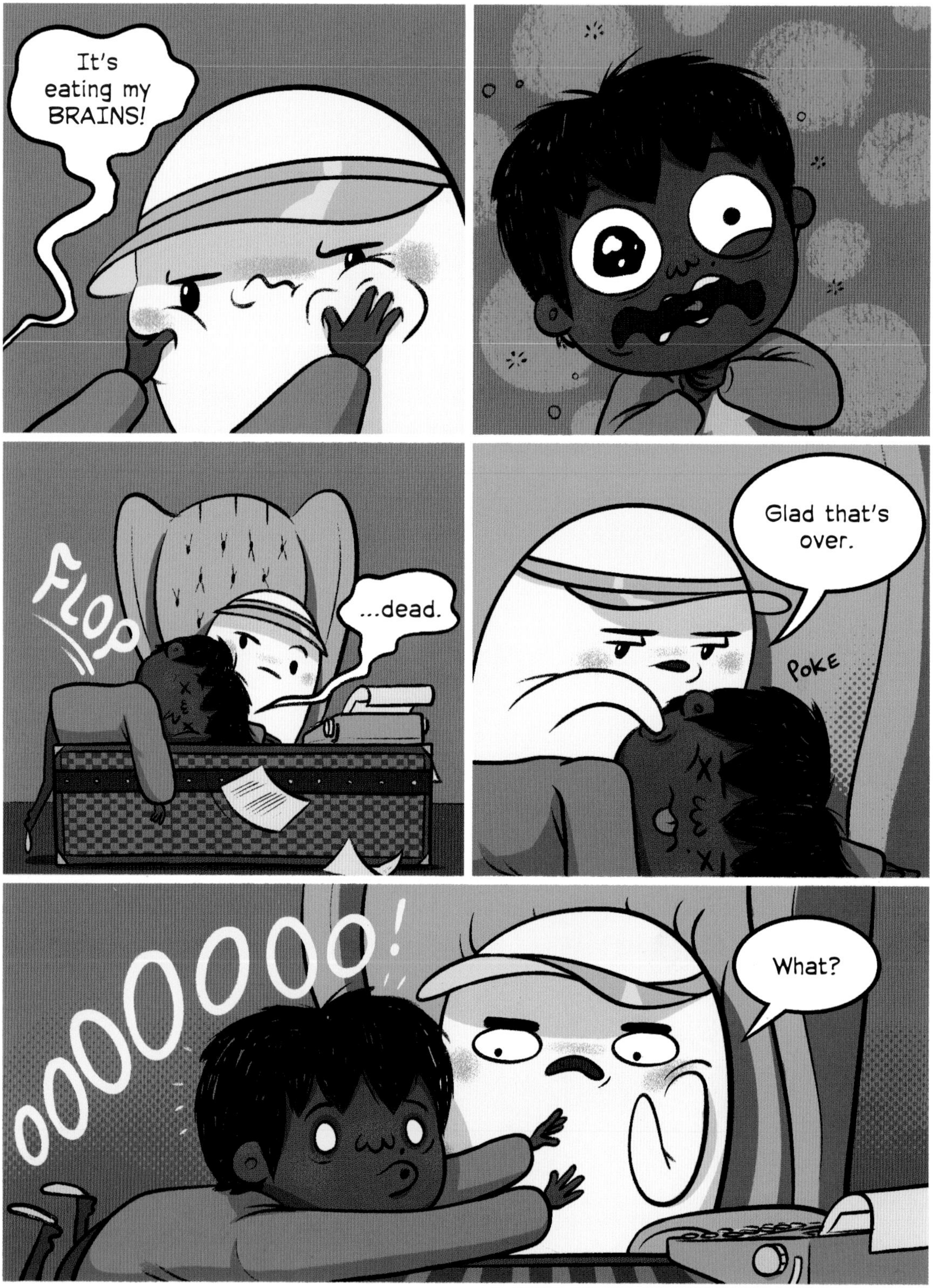
It's eating my BRAINS!
FLOP
...dead.
Glad that's over.
POKE
OOOOOOOOO!
What?

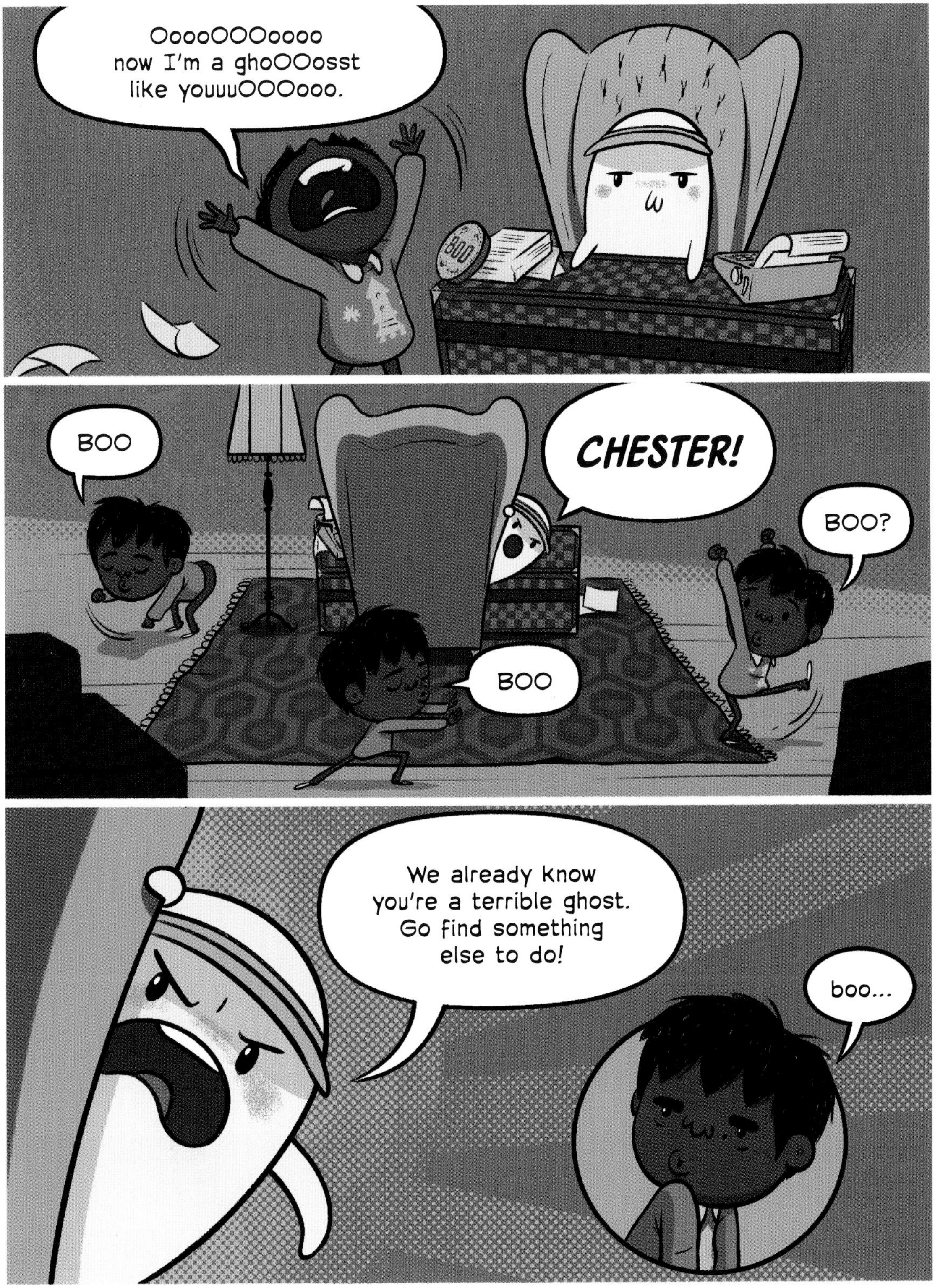
OoooOOOoooo
now I'm a ghoOOosst
like youuuOOOooo.
BOO
CHESTER!
BOO?
BOO
We already know
you're a terrible ghost.
Go find something
else to do!
boo...

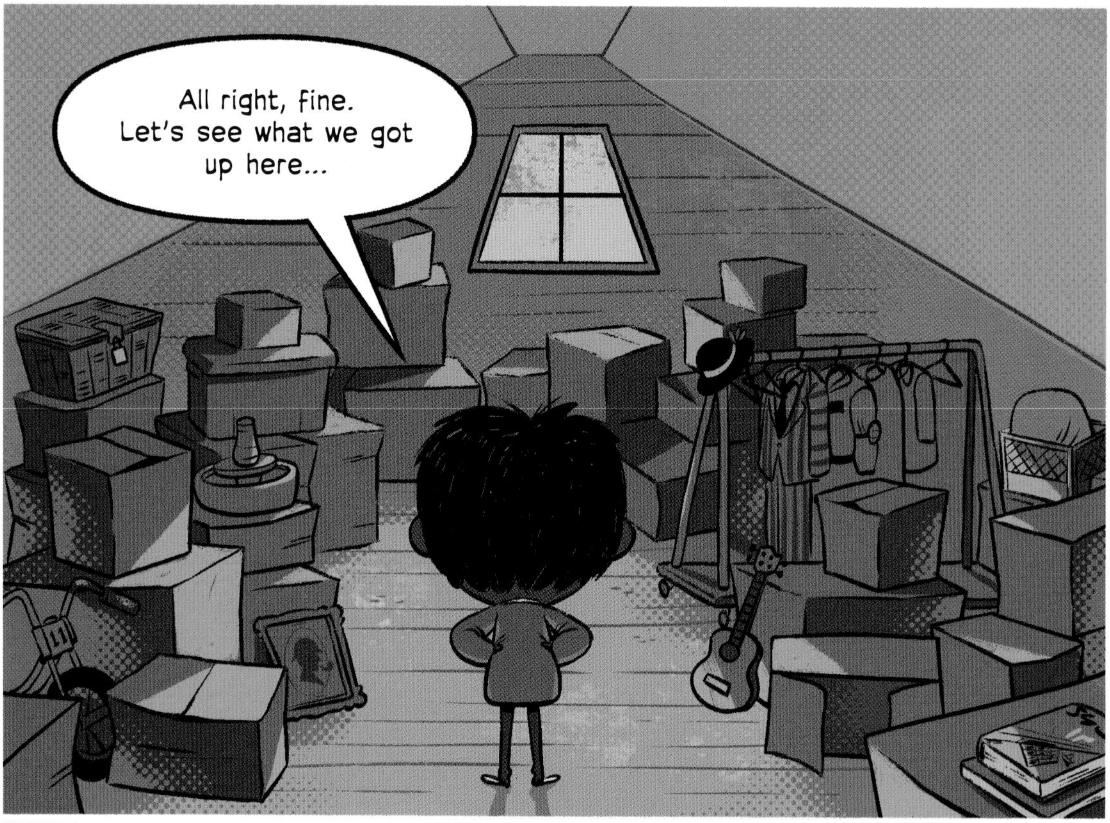
All right, fine.
Let's see what we got up here...

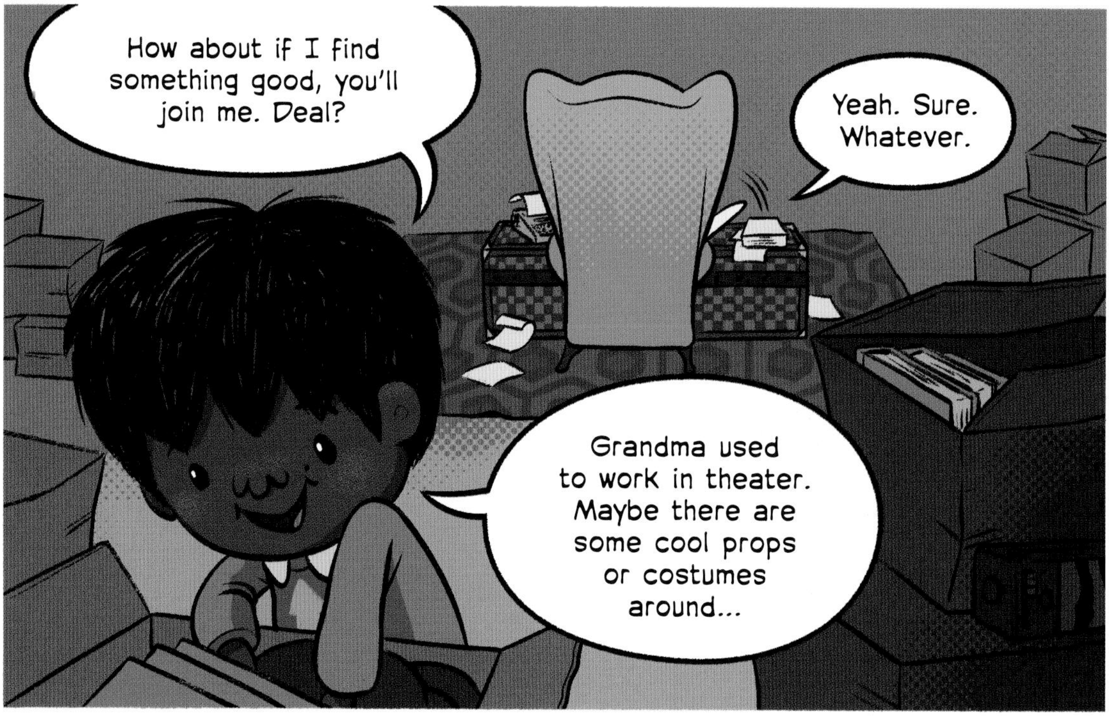
How about if I find something good, you'll join me. Deal?
Yeah. Sure. Whatever.
Grandma used to work in theater. Maybe there are some cool props or costumes around...

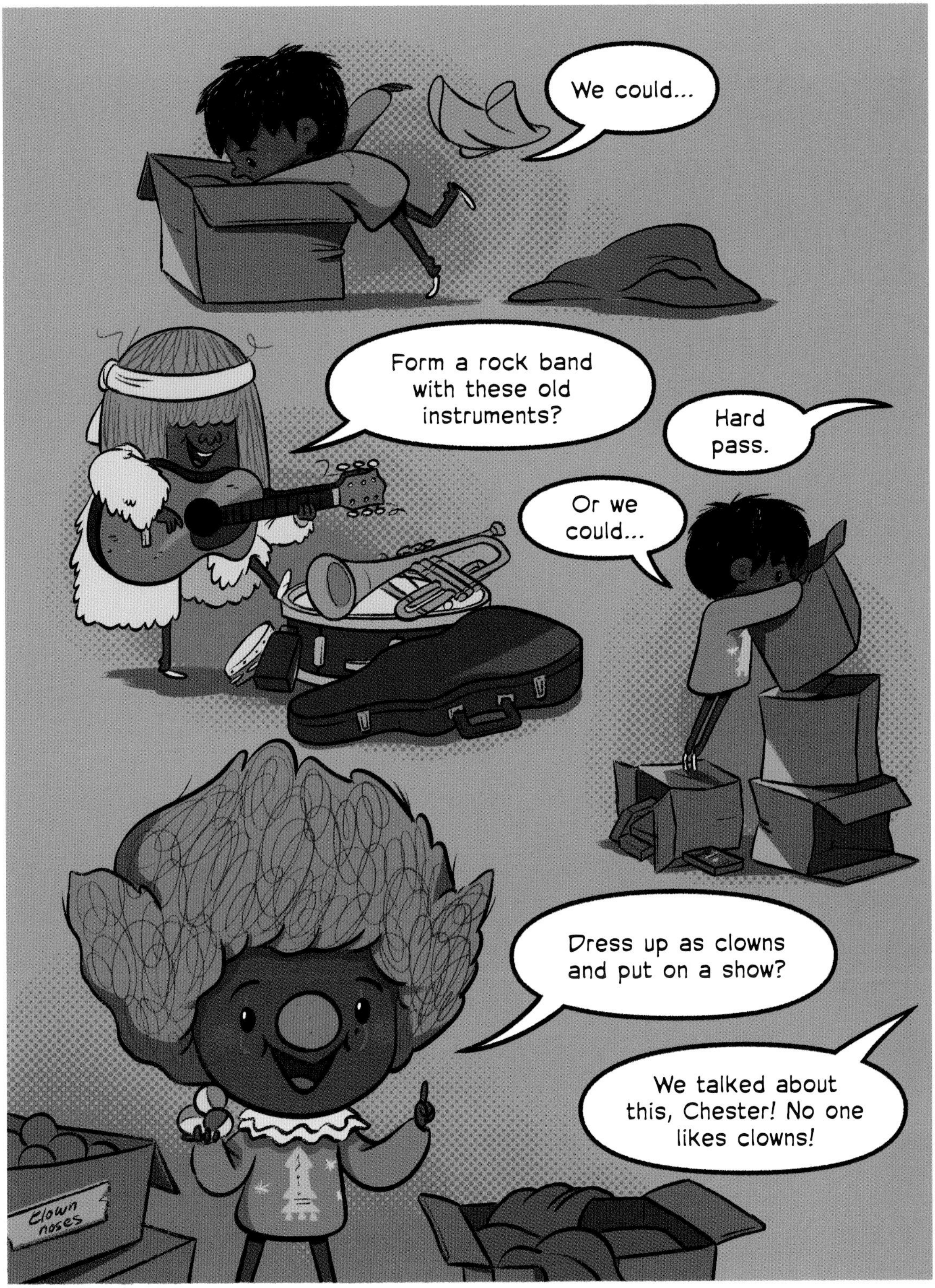
We could...
Form a rock band with these old instruments?
Hard pass.
Or we could...
Dress up as clowns and put on a show?
We talked about this, Chester! No one likes clowns!
Clown noses

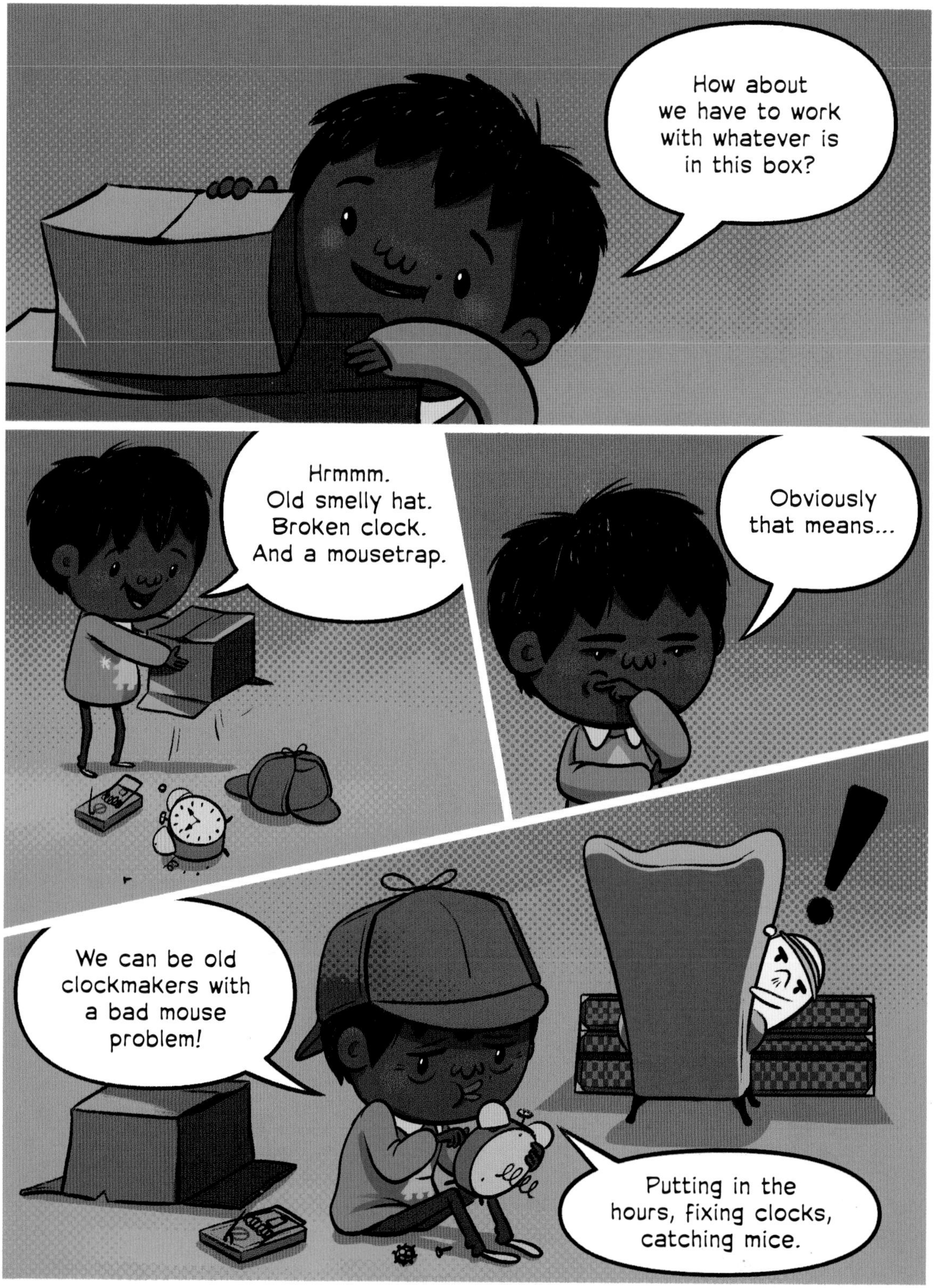
How about we have to work with whatever is in this box?
Hrmmm. Old smelly hat. Broken clock. And a mousetrap.
Obviously that means...
We can be old clockmakers with a bad mouse problem!
Putting in the hours, fixing clocks, catching mice.

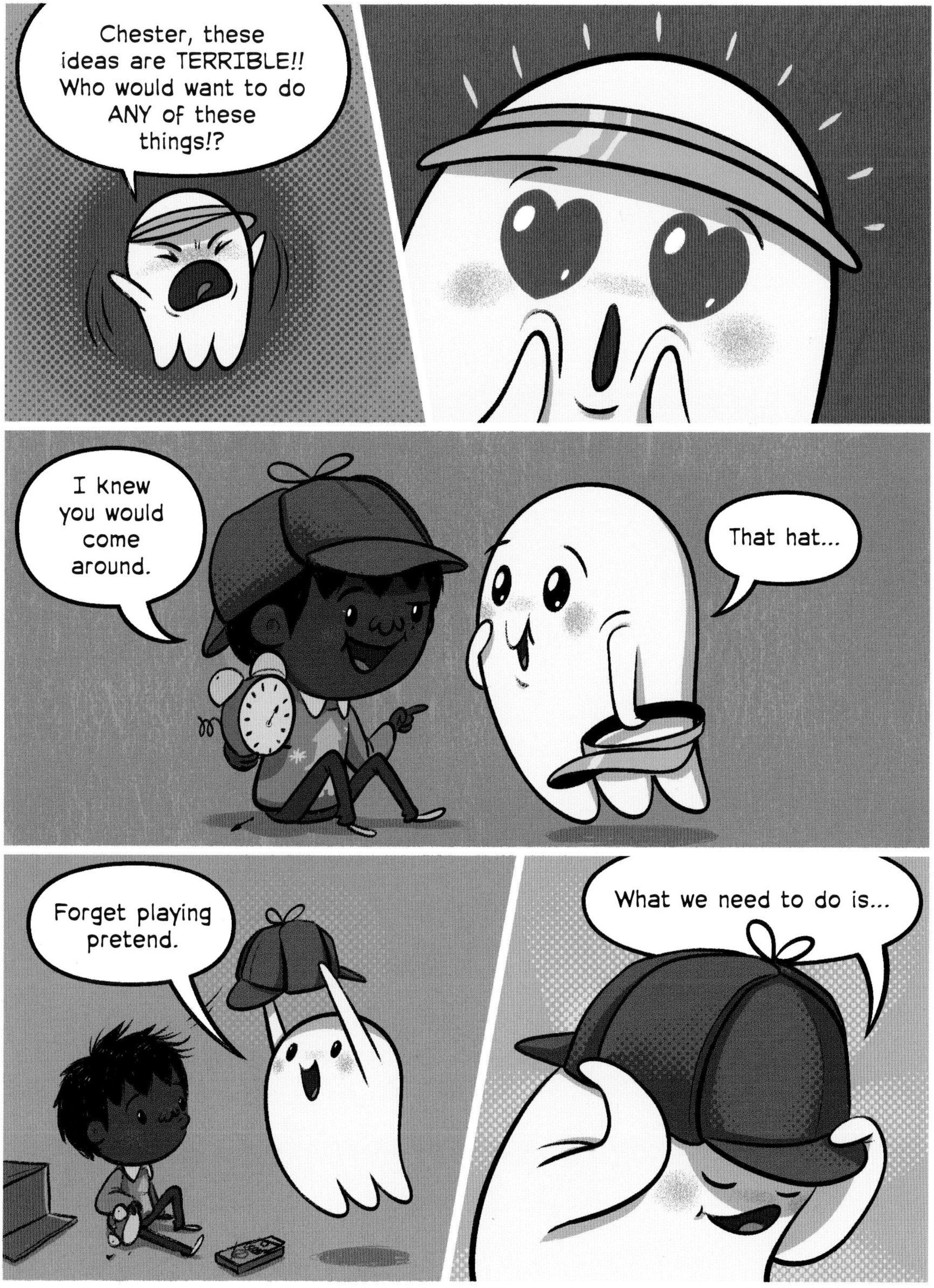
Chester, these ideas are TERRIBLE!! Who would want to do ANY of these things!?
I knew you would come around.
That hat...
Forget playing pretend.
What we need to do is...

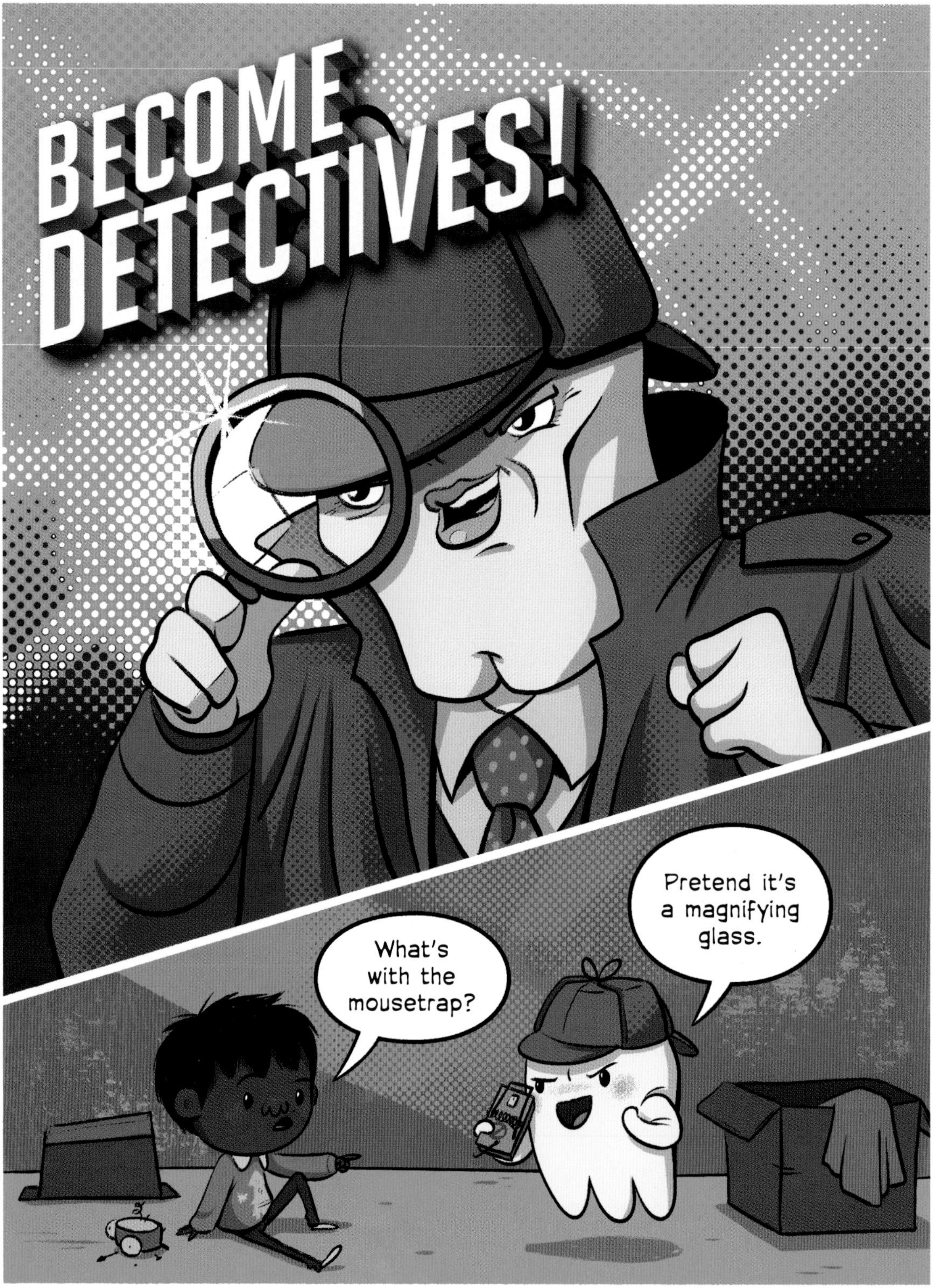
BECOME DETECTIVES!
What's with the mousetrap?
Pretend it's a magnifying glass.

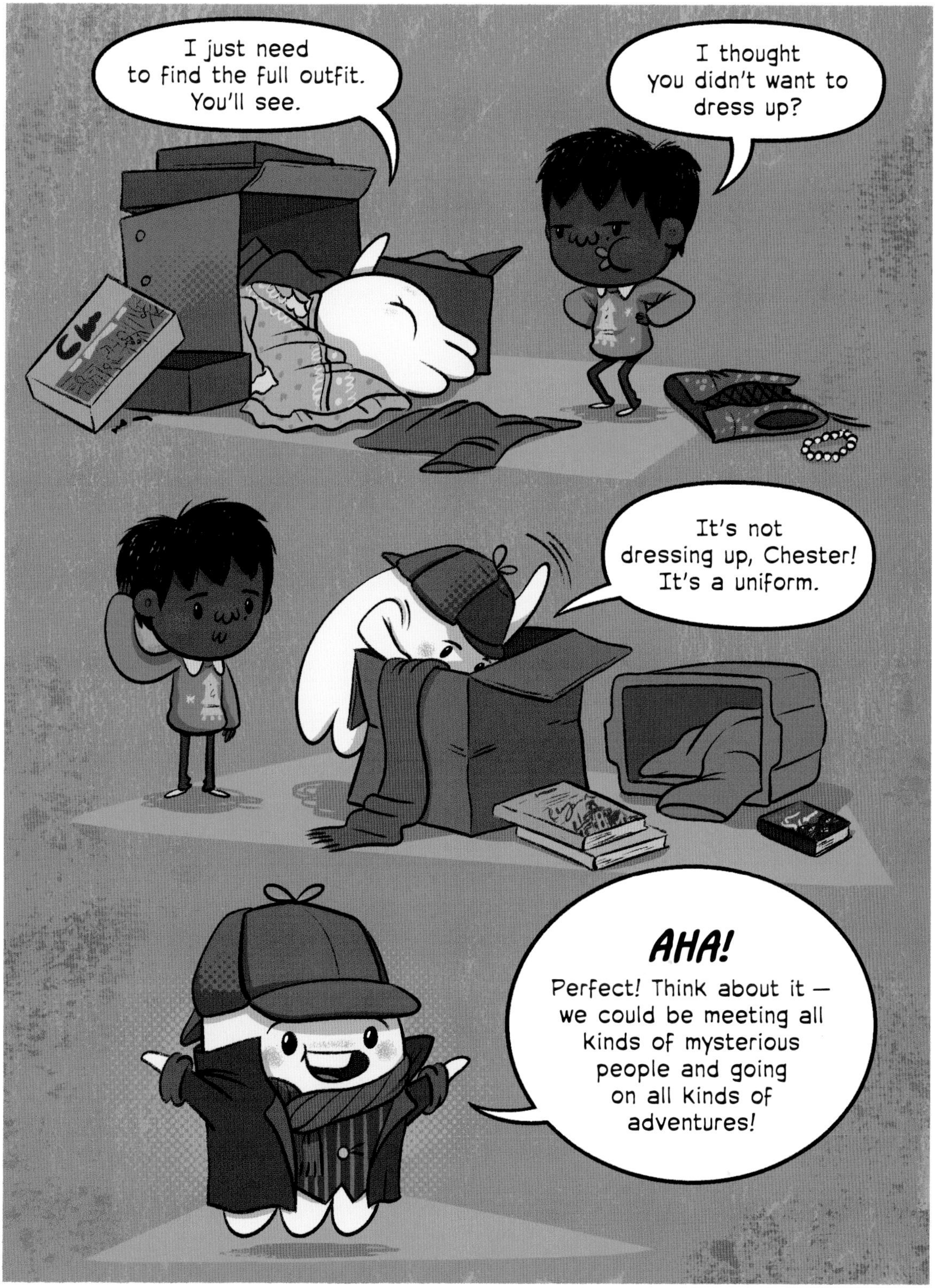
I just need to find the full outfit. You'll see.
I thought you didn't want to dress up?
It's not dressing up, Chester! It's a uniform.
AHA!
Perfect! Think about it — we could be meeting all kinds of mysterious people and going on all kinds of adventures!

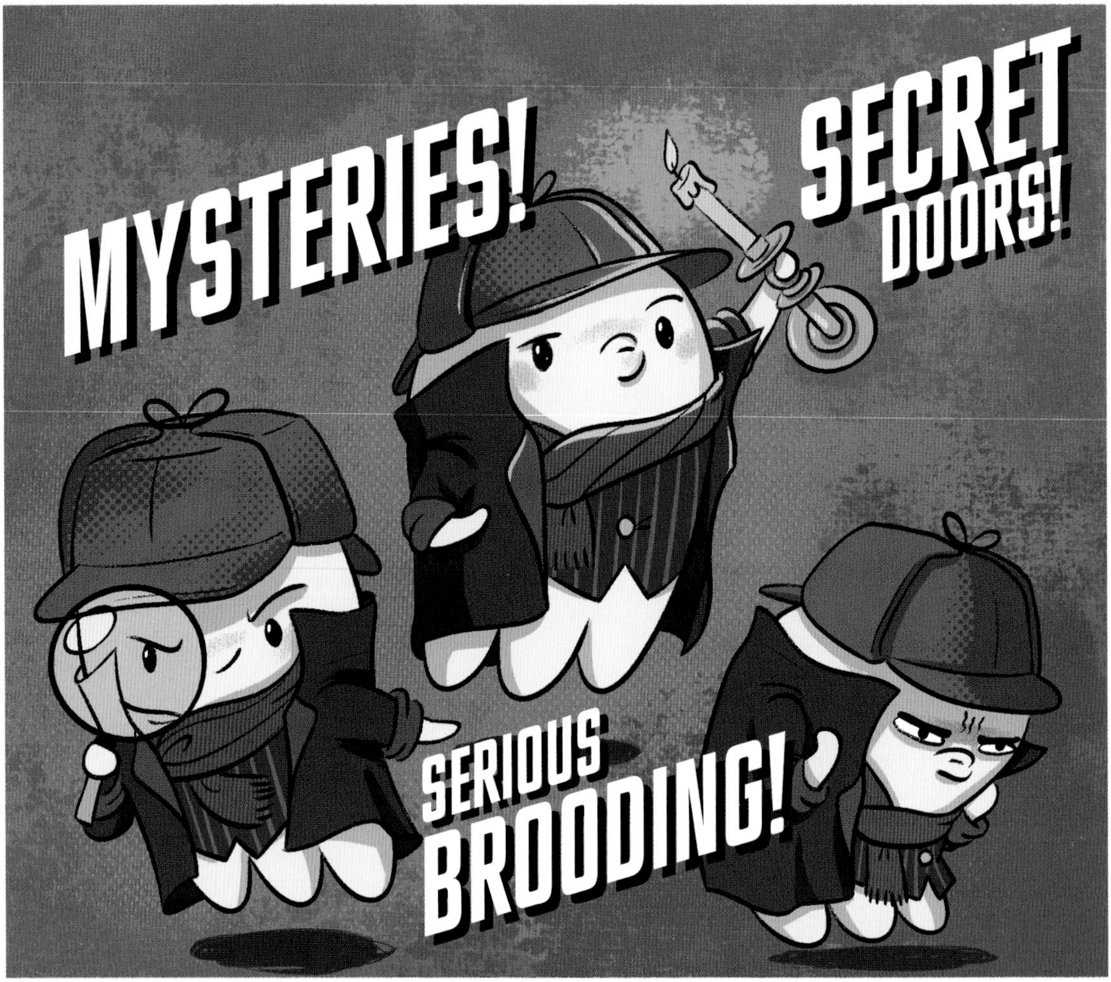
MYSTERIES!
SECRET DOORS!
SERIOUS BROODING!

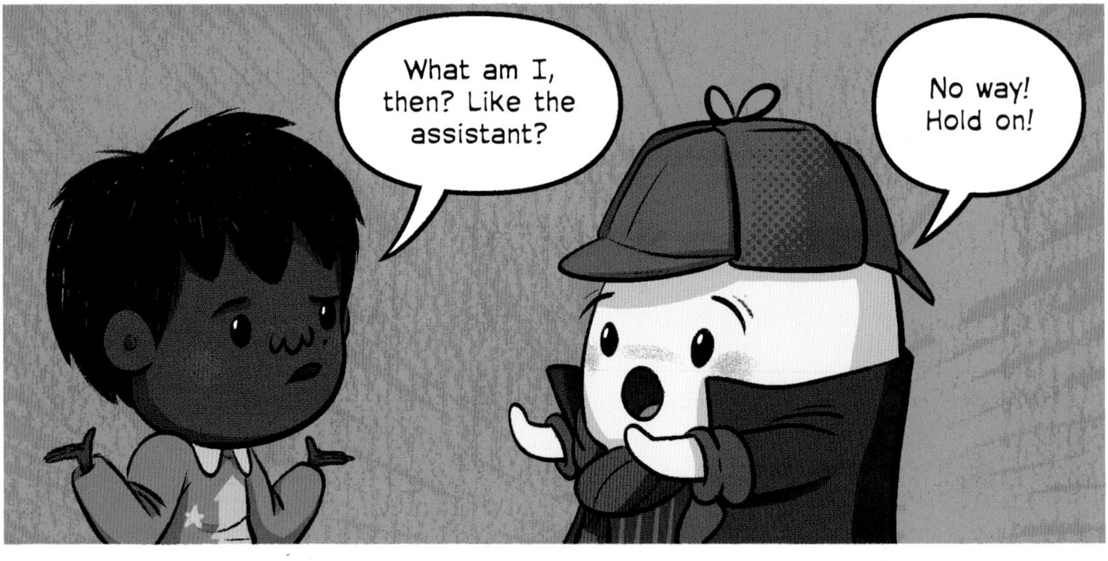
What am I, then? Like the assistant?
No way! Hold on!

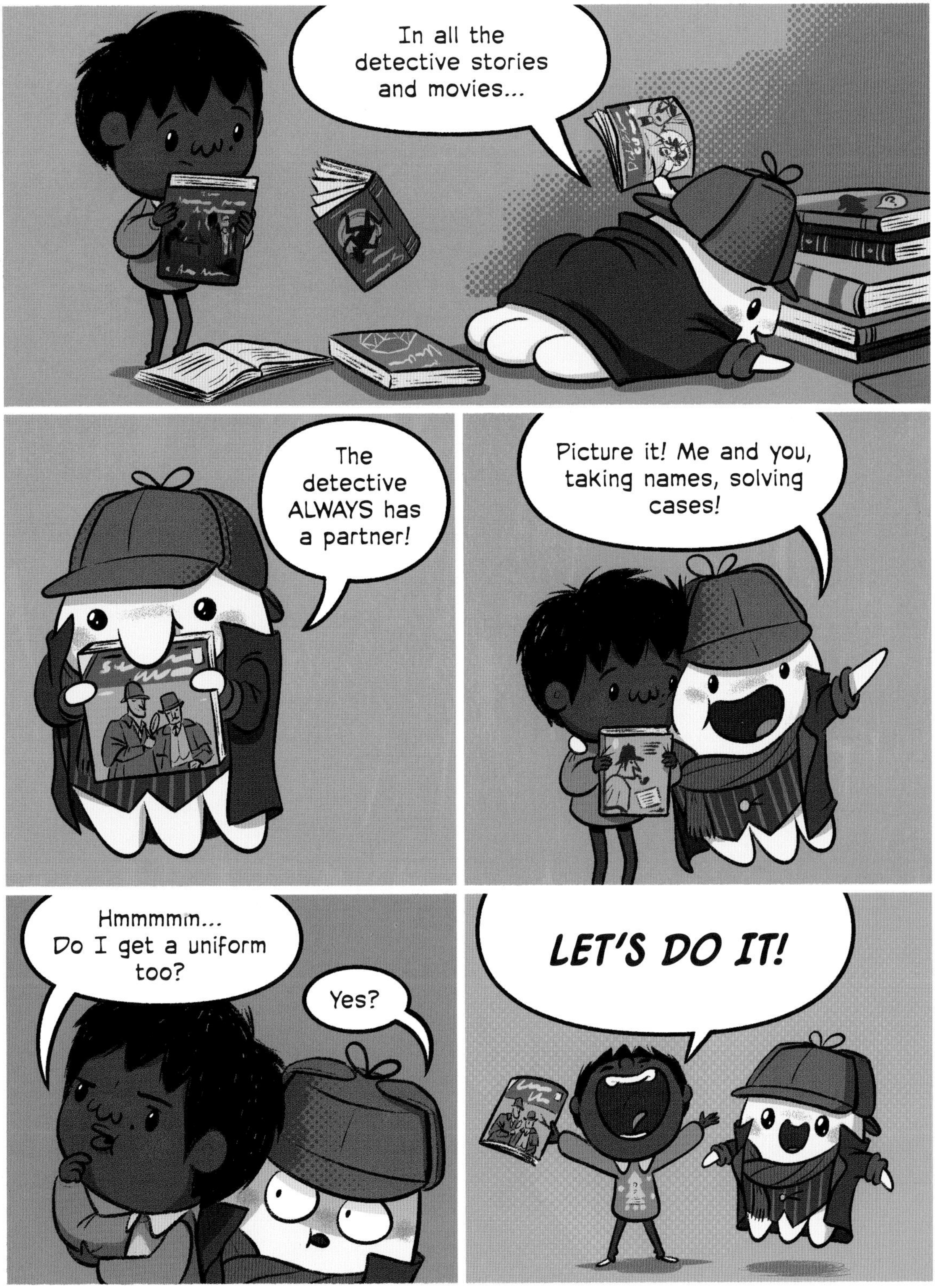
In all the detective stories and movies...
The detective ALWAYS has a partner!
Picture it! Me and you, taking names, solving cases!
Hmmmmm... Do I get a uniform too?
Yes?
LET'S DO IT!

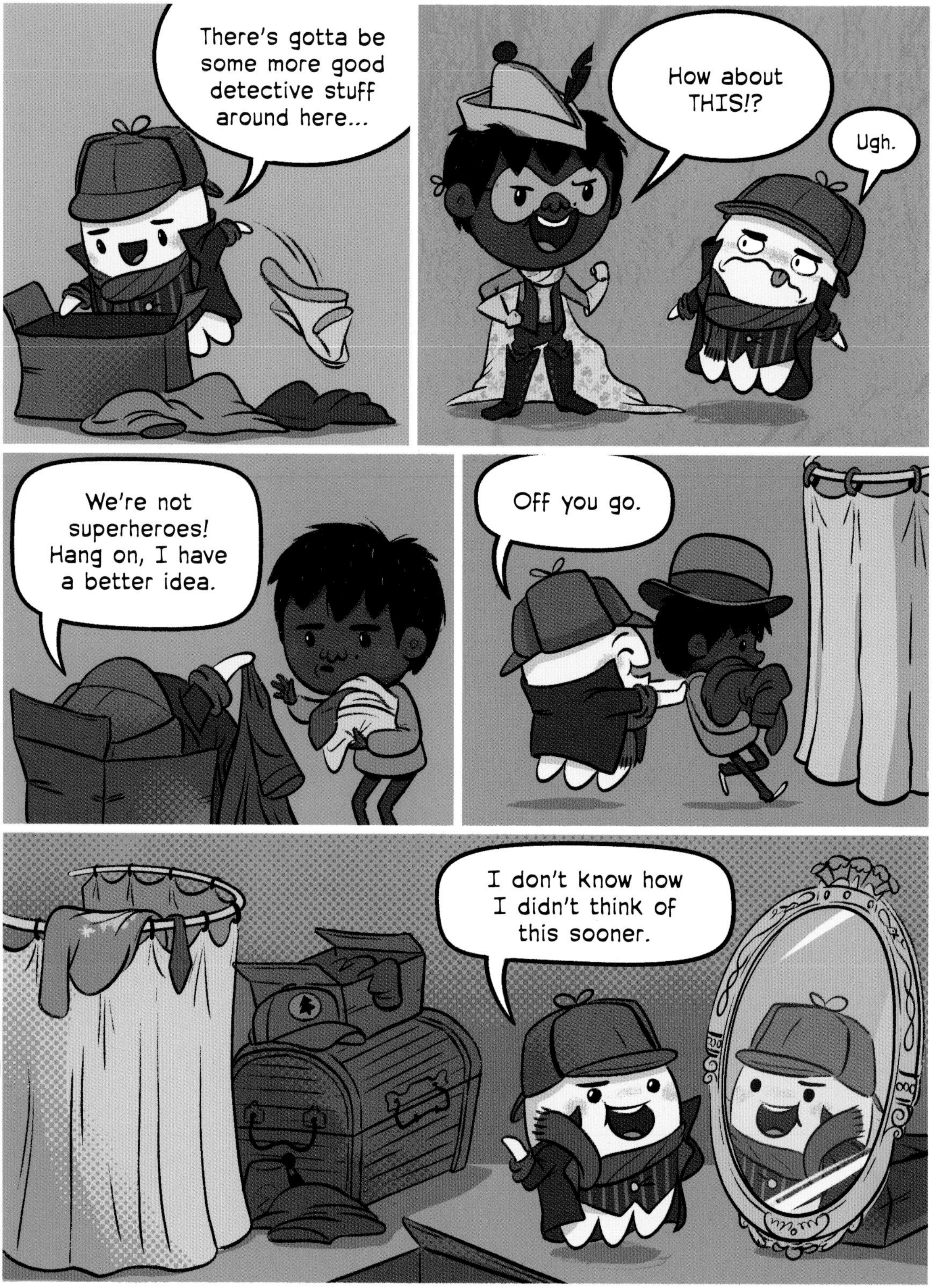
There's gotta be some more good detective stuff around here...
How about THIS!?
Ugh.
We're not superheroes! Hang on, I have a better idea.
Off you go.
I don't know how I didn't think of this sooner.

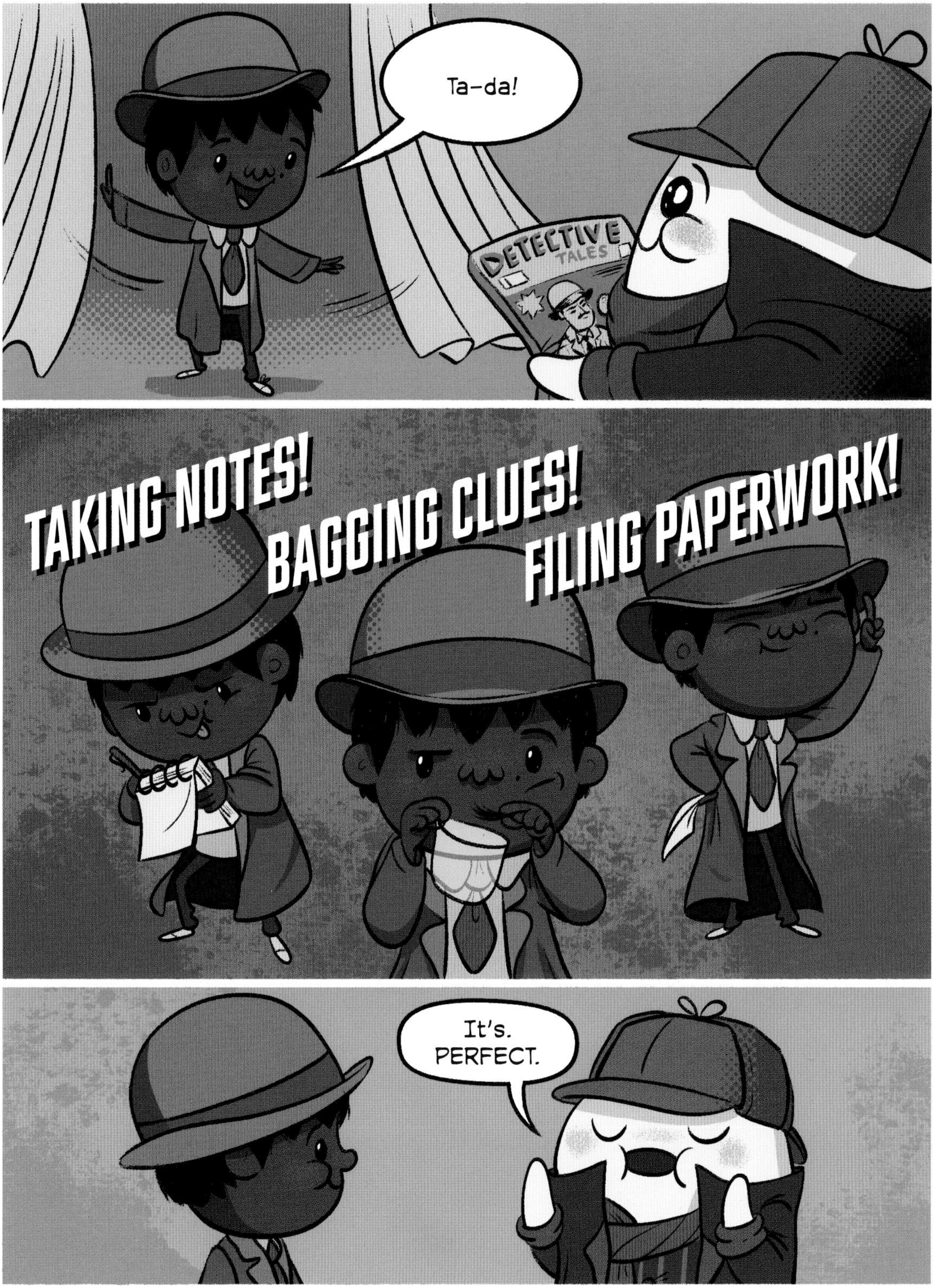
Ta-da!
DETECTIVE TALES
TAKING NOTES!
BAGGING CLUES!
FILING PAPERWORK!
It's. PERFECT.

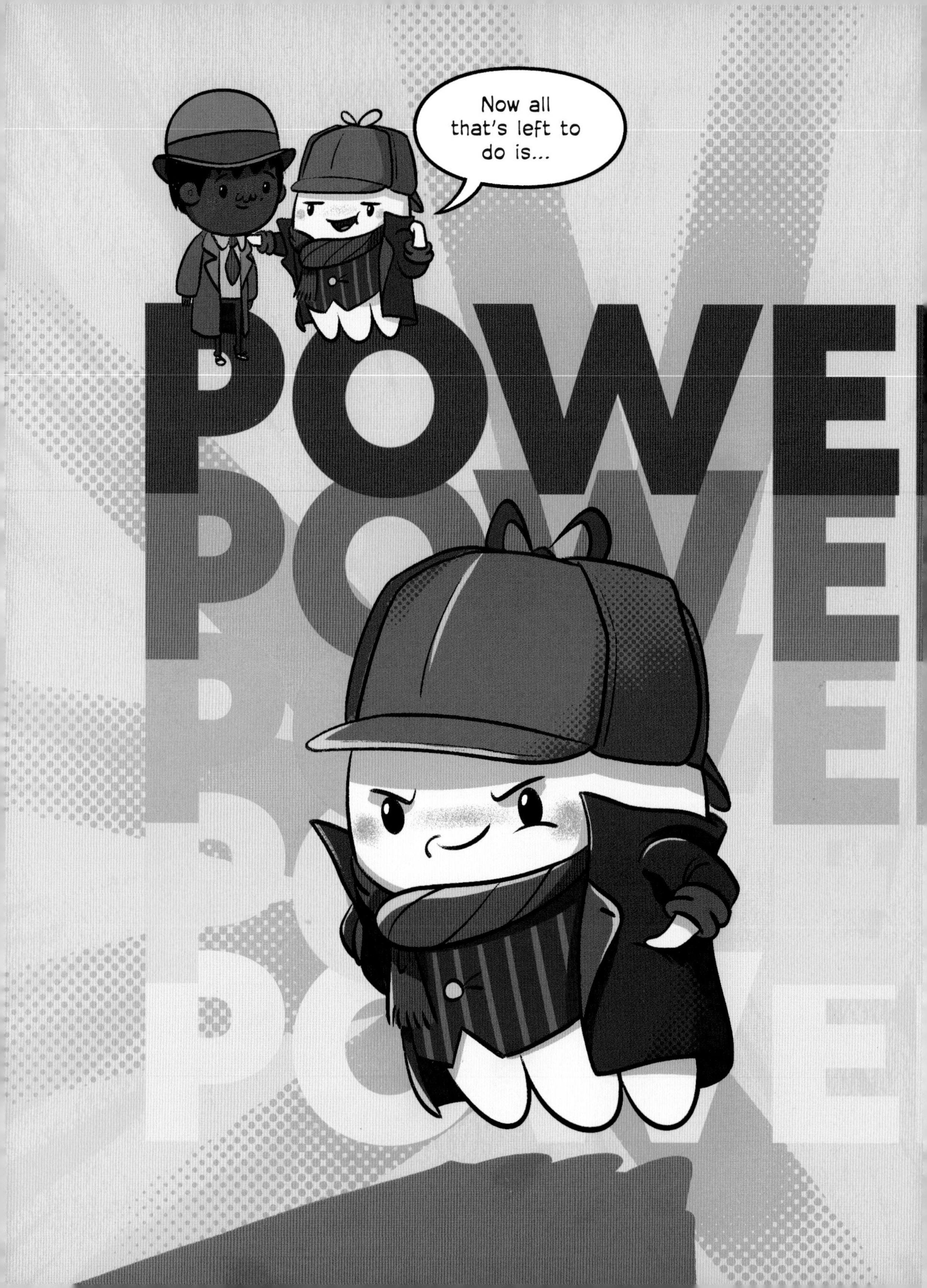
Now all that's left to do is...
POWE
POWE
POWE
POWE

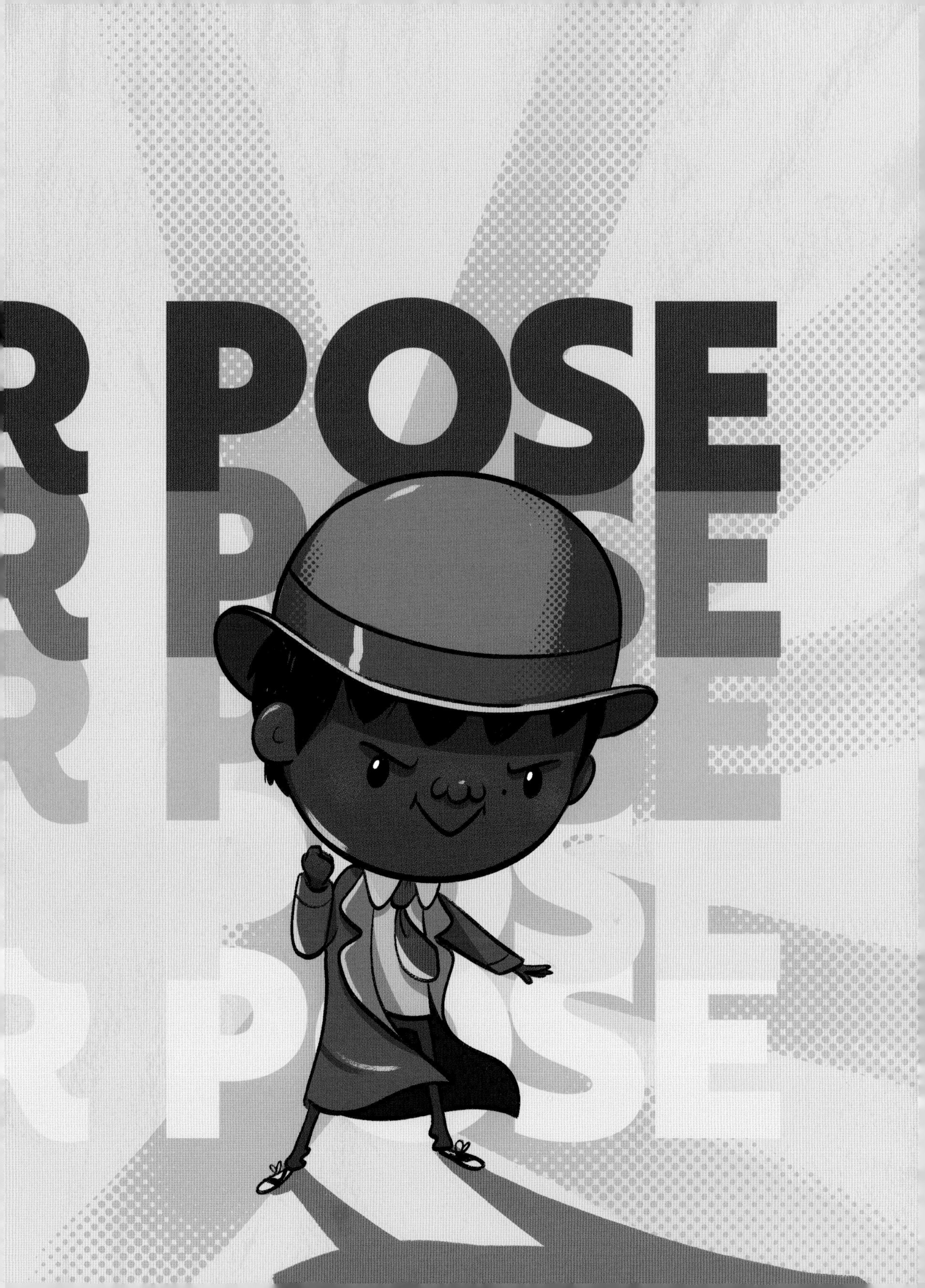
R POSE

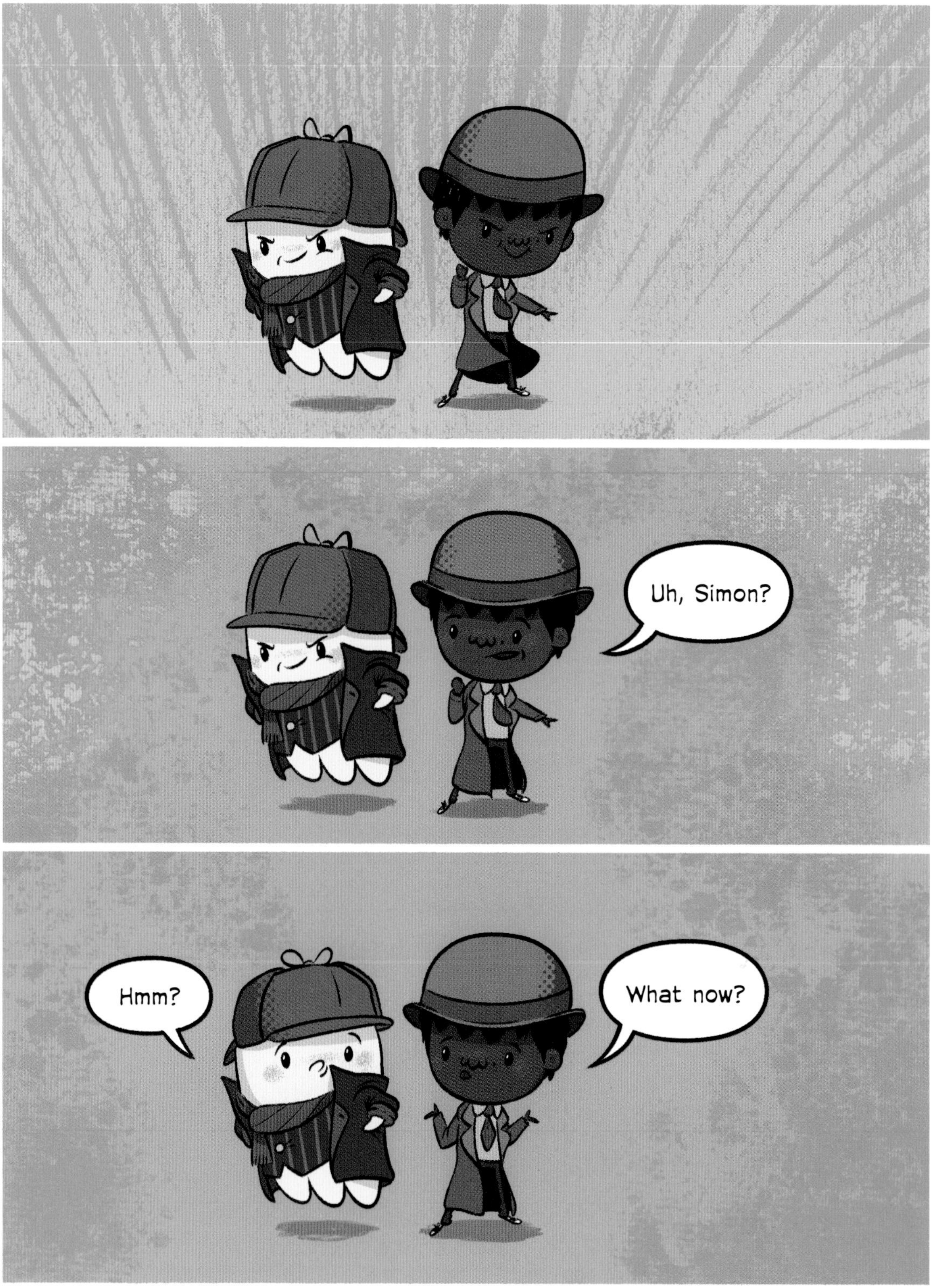
Uh, Simon?
Hmm?
What now?

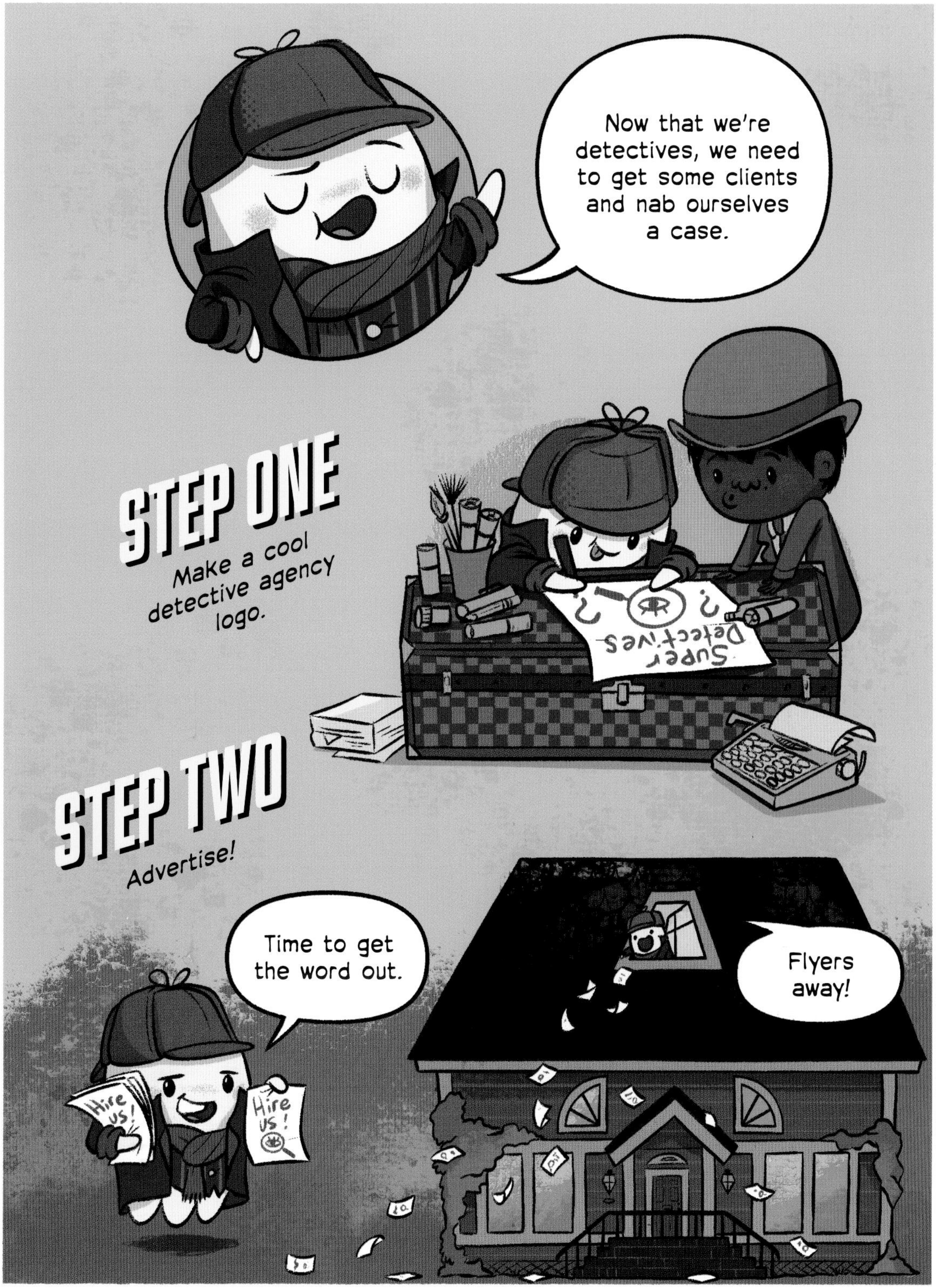
Now that we're detectives, we need to get some clients and nab ourselves a case.
STEP ONE
Make a cool detective agency logo.
Super Detectives
STEP TWO
Advertise!
Time to get the word out.
Hire us!
Hire us!
Flyers away!

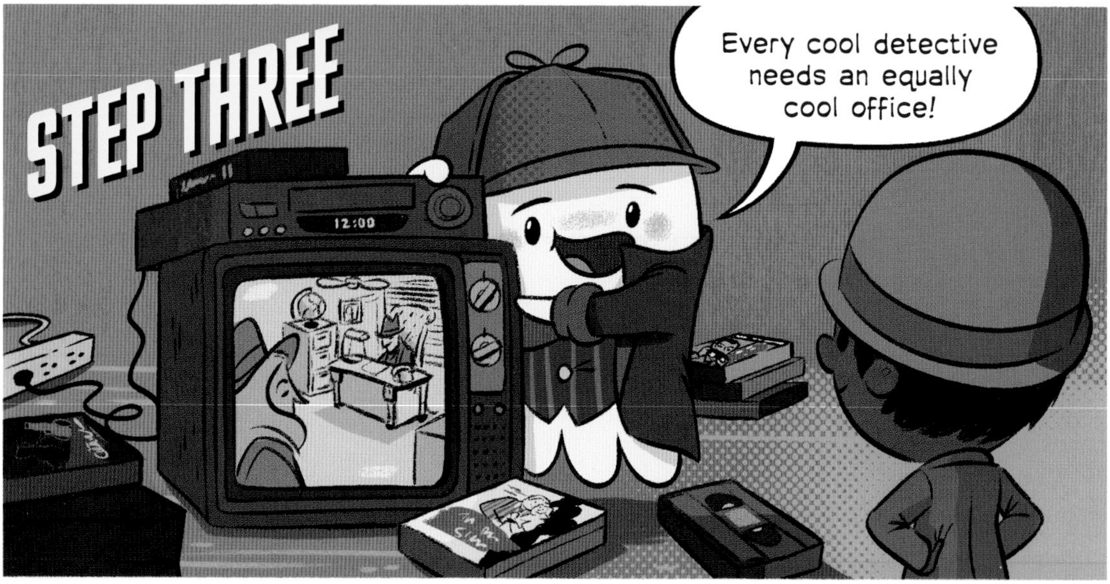
STEP THREE
Every cool detective needs an equally cool office!

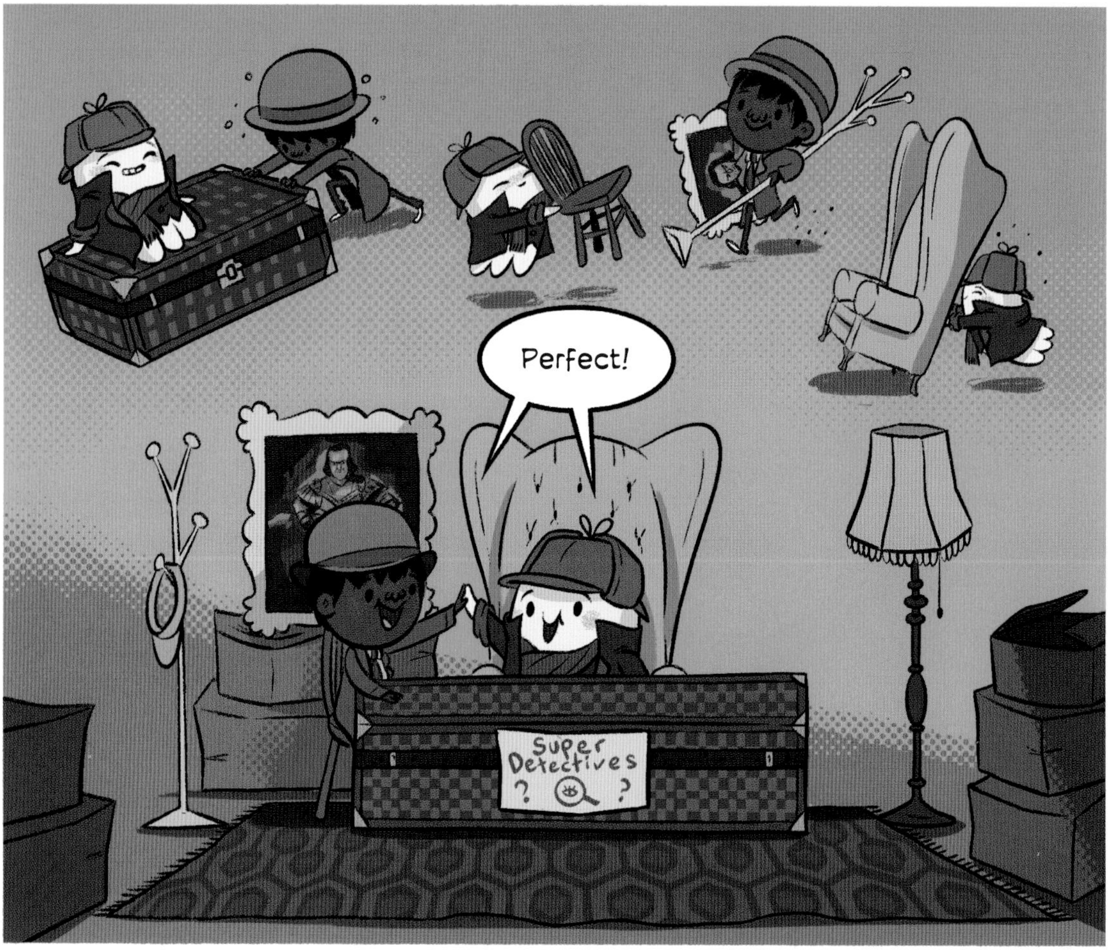
Perfect!
Super Detectives

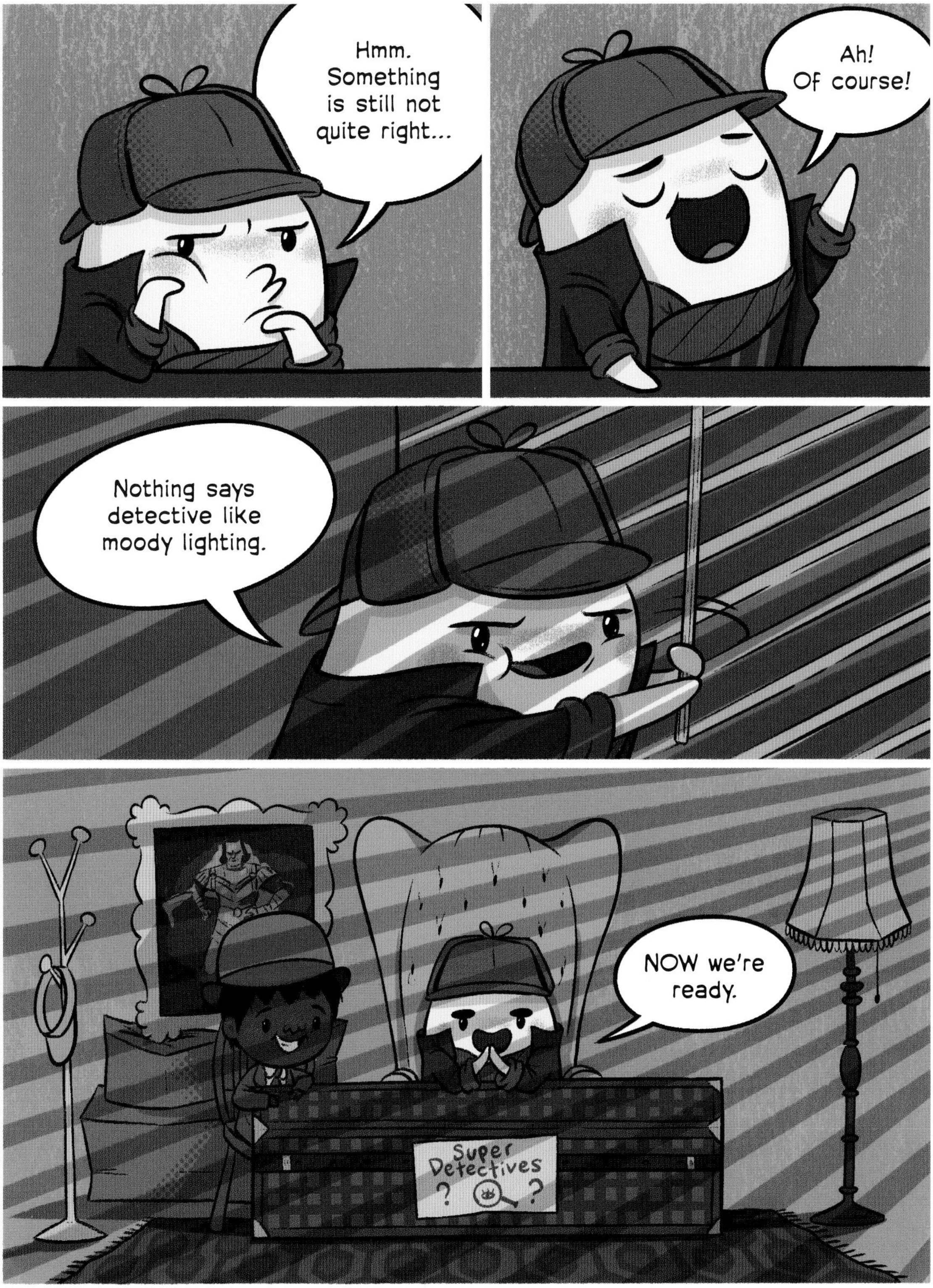
Hmm. Something is still not quite right...
Ah! Of course!
Nothing says detective like moody lighting.
NOW we're ready.
Super Detectives

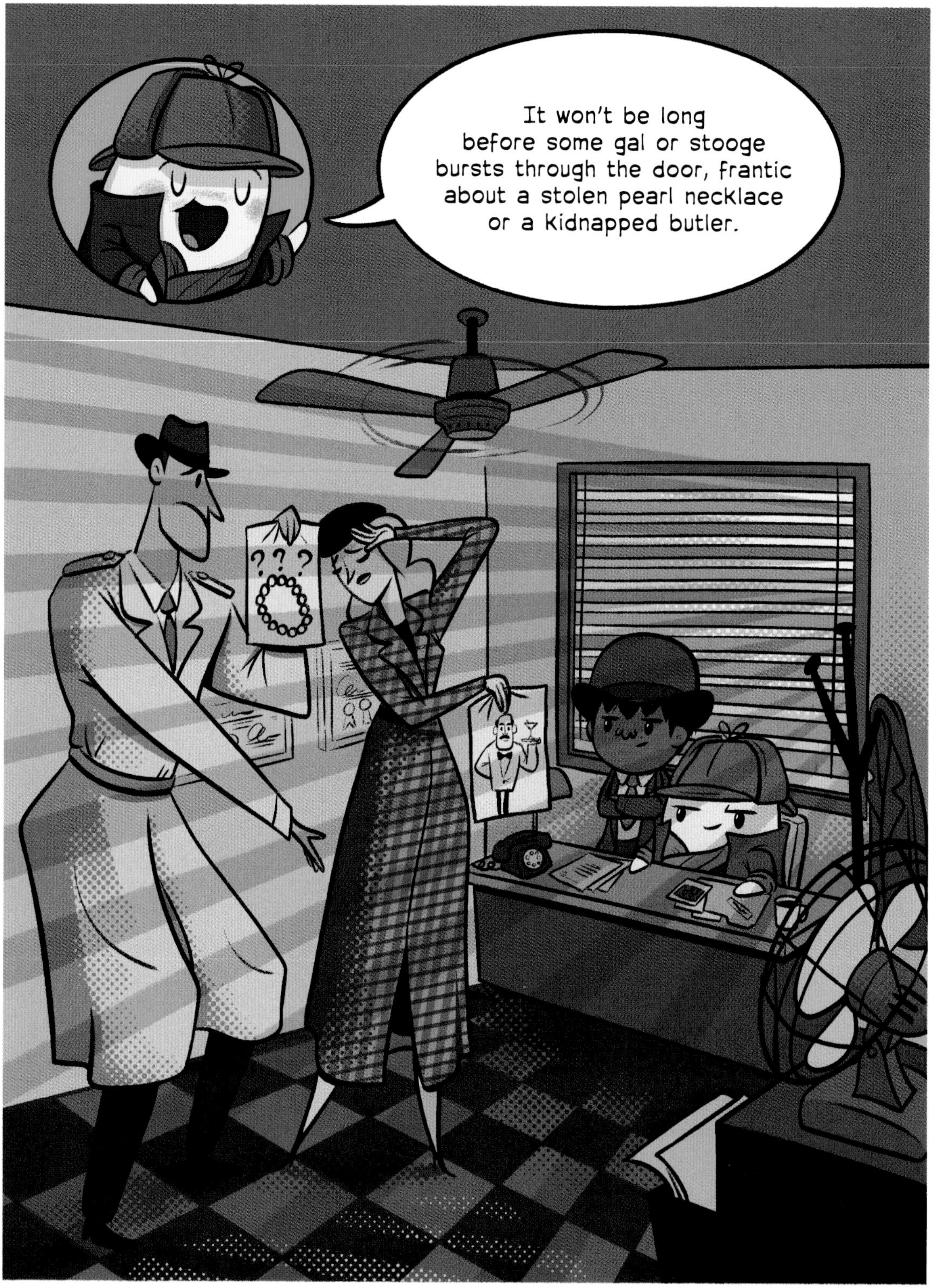
It won't be long before some gal or stooge bursts through the door, frantic about a stolen pearl necklace or a kidnapped butler.

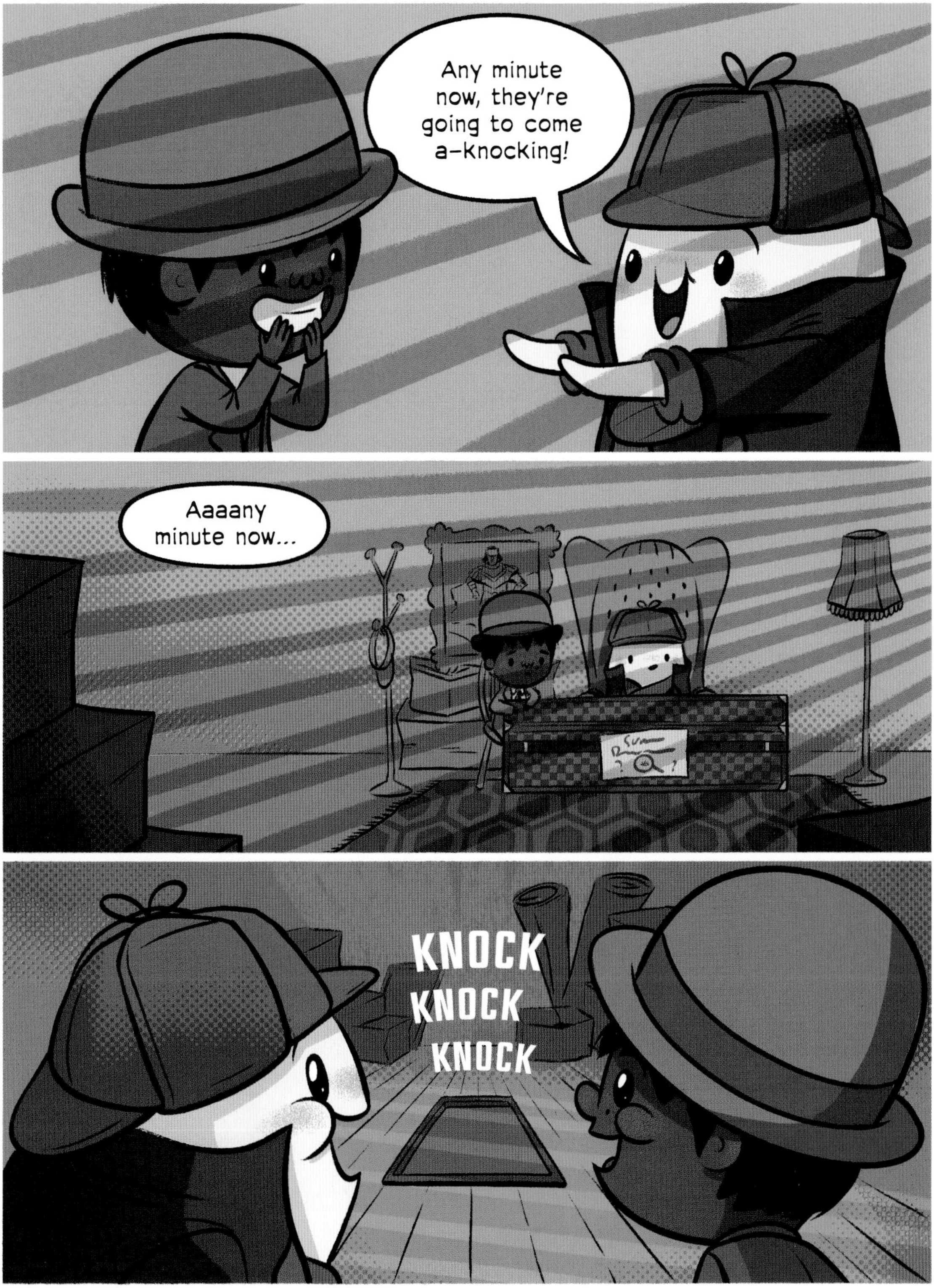
Any minute now, they're going to come a-knocking!
Aaaany minute now...
KNOCK
KNOCK
KNOCK

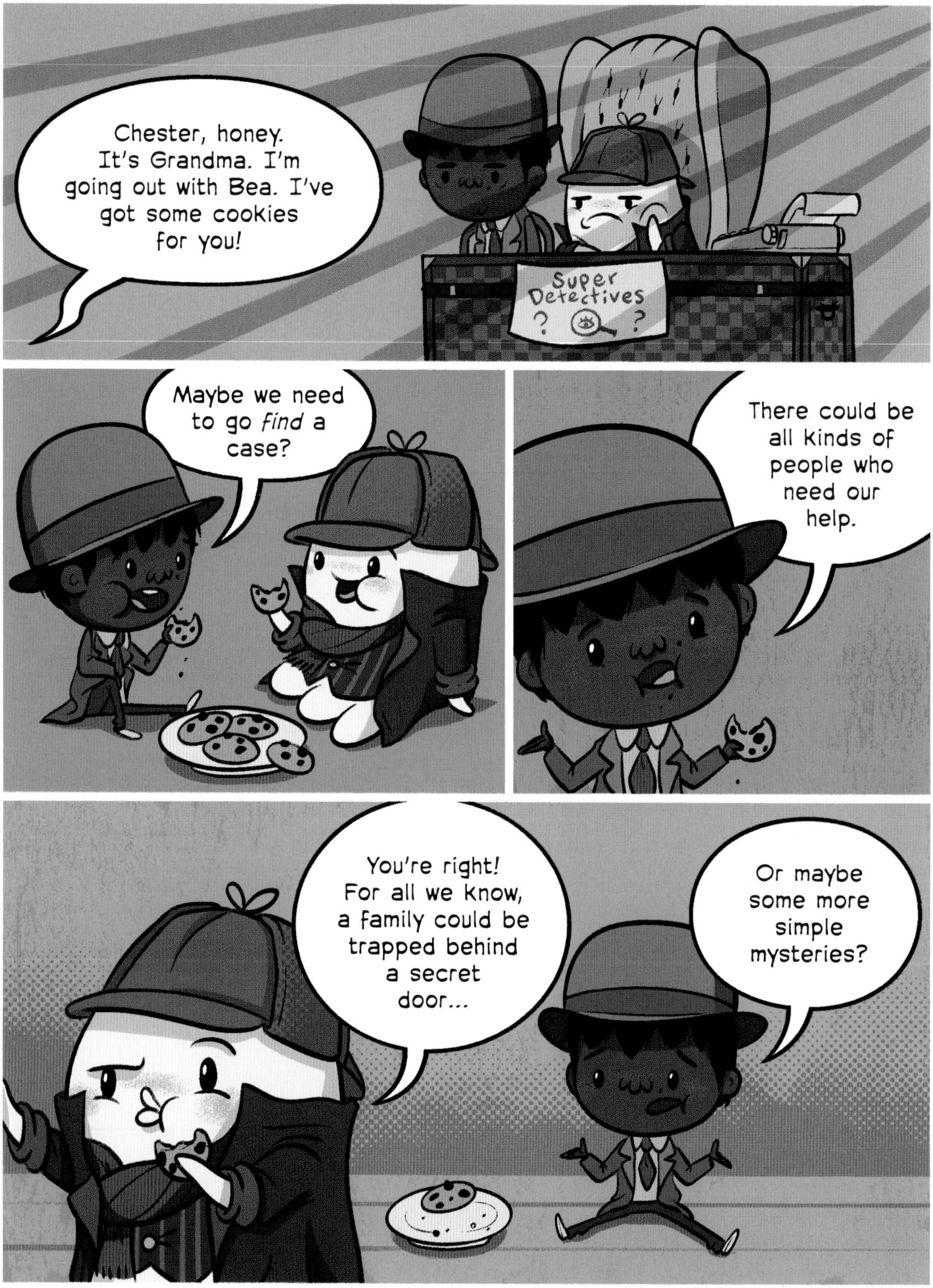
Chester, honey. It's Grandma. I'm going out with Bea. I've got some cookies for you!
Super Detectives
Maybe we need to go *find* a case?
There could be all kinds of people who need our help.
You're right! For all we know, a family could be trapped behind a secret door...
Or maybe some more simple mysteries?

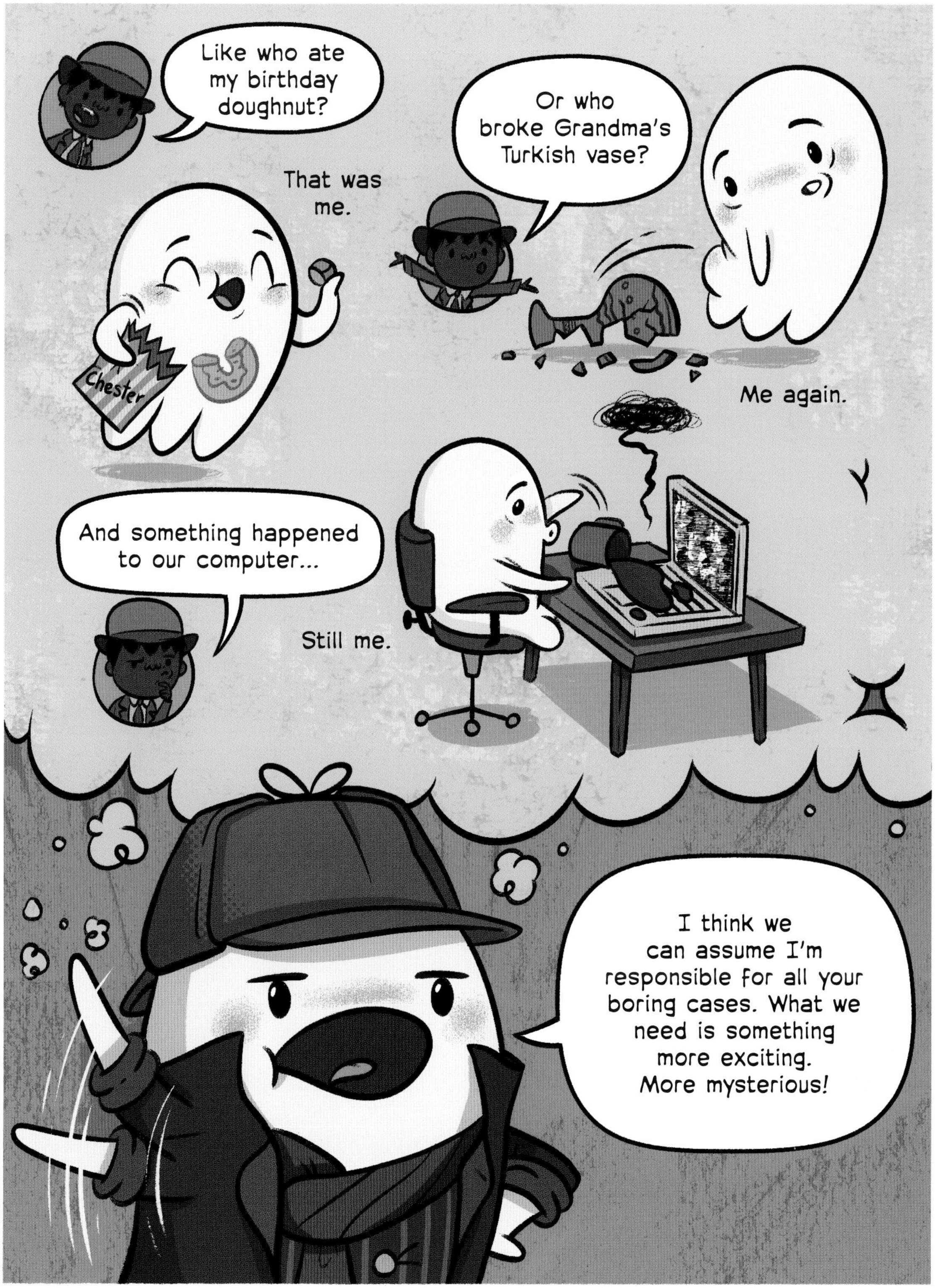
Like who ate my birthday doughnut?
That was me.
Chester
Or who broke Grandma's Turkish vase?
Me again.
And something happened to our computer...
Still me.
I think we can assume I'm responsible for all your boring cases. What we need is something more exciting. More mysterious!

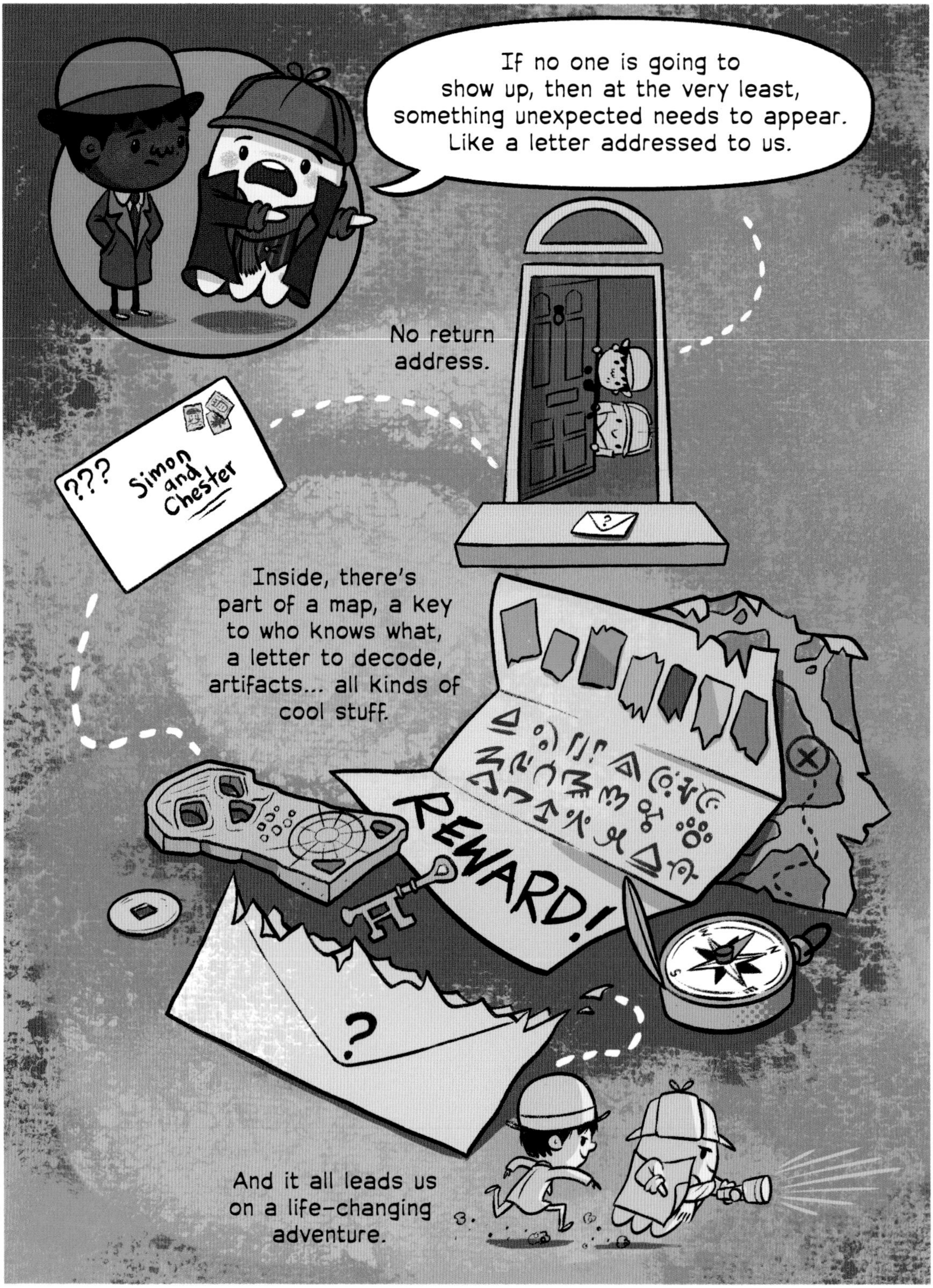
If no one is going to show up, then at the very least, something unexpected needs to appear. Like a letter addressed to us.
No return address.
??? Simon and Chester
Inside, there's part of a map, a key to who knows what, a letter to decode, artifacts... all kinds of cool stuff.
REWARD!
And it all leads us on a life-changing adventure.

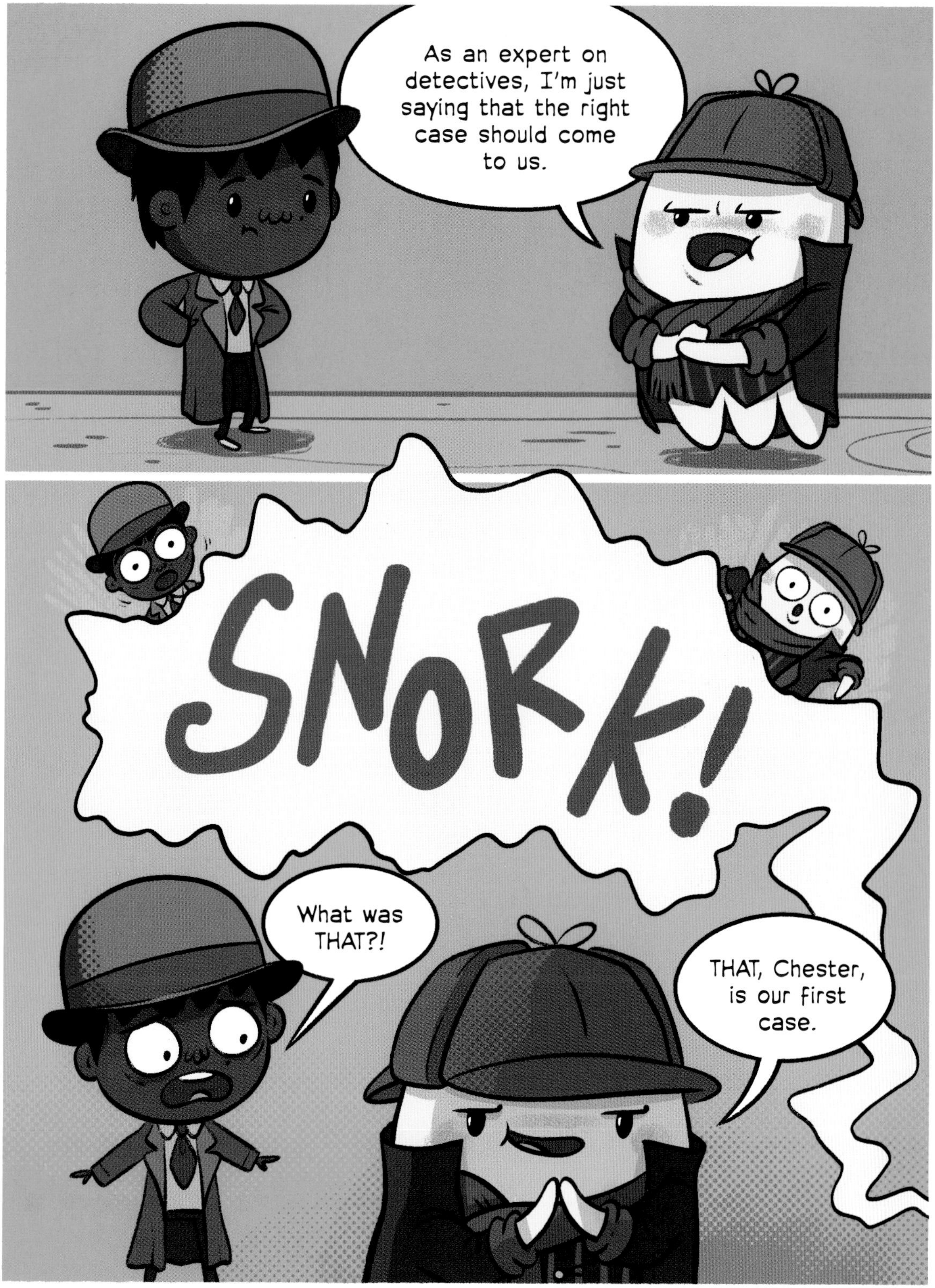
As an expert on detectives, I'm just saying that the right case should come to us.
SNORK!
What was THAT?!
THAT, Chester, is our first case.

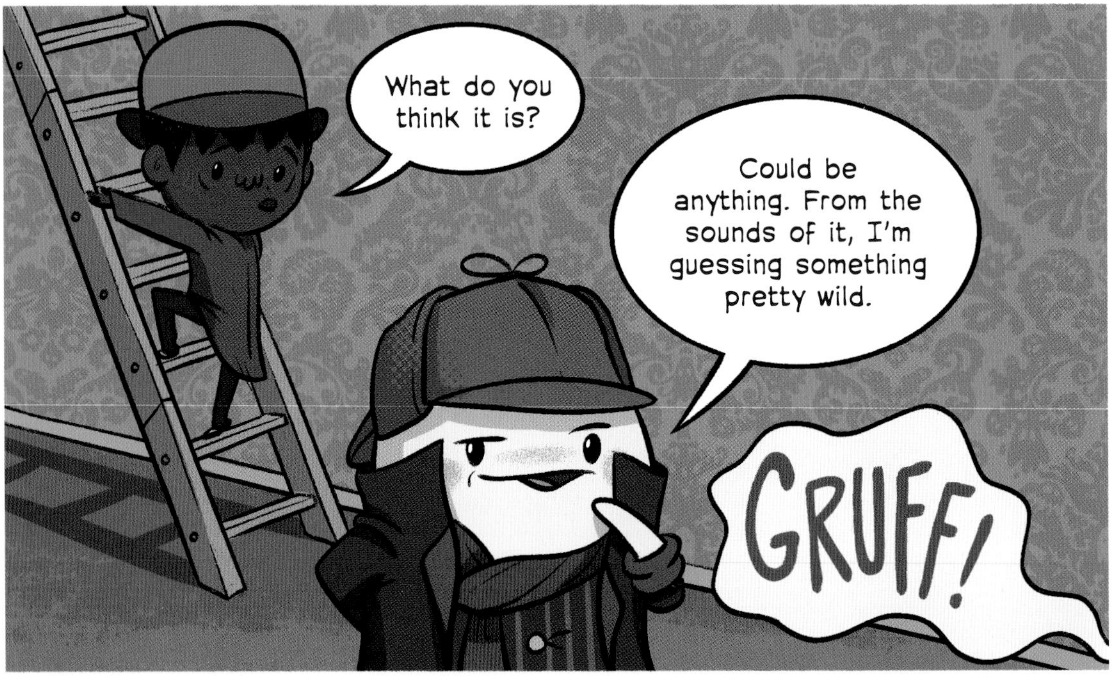
What do you think it is?
Could be anything. From the sounds of it, I'm guessing something pretty wild.
GRUFF!

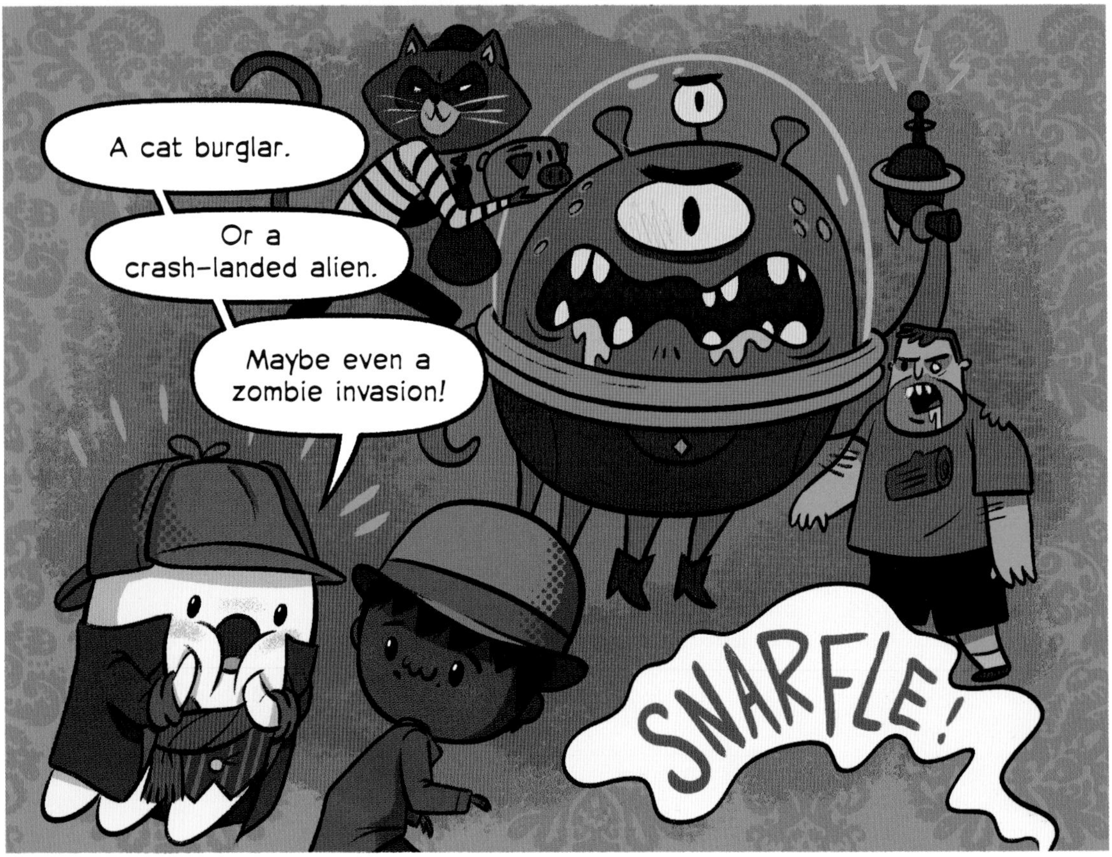
A cat burglar.
Or a crash-landed alien.
Maybe even a zombie invasion!
SNARFLE!

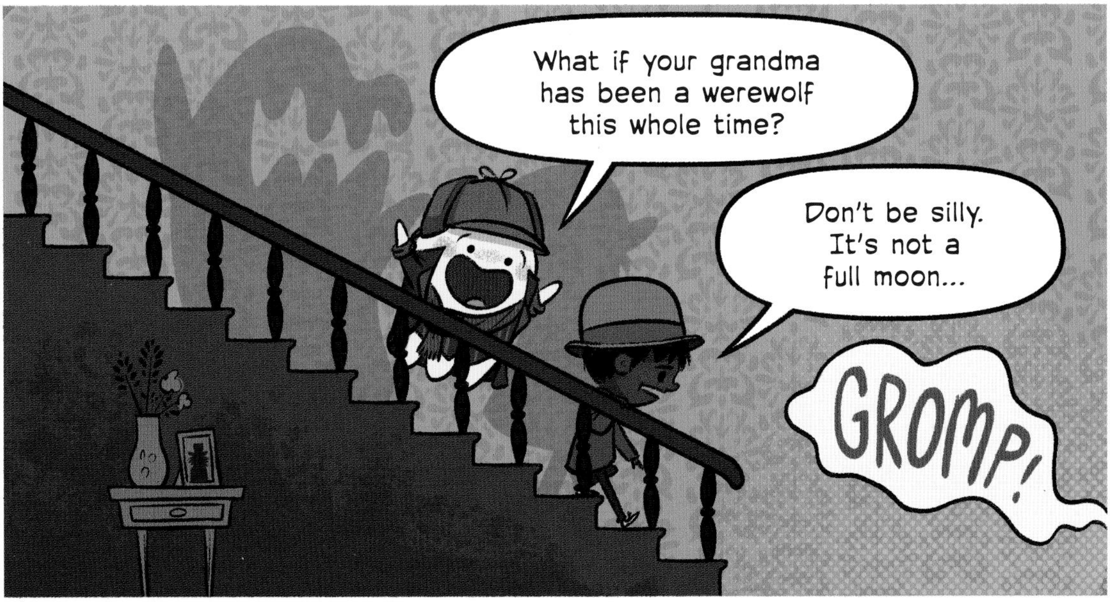
What if your grandma has been a werewolf this whole time?
Don't be silly. It's not a full moon...
GROMP!

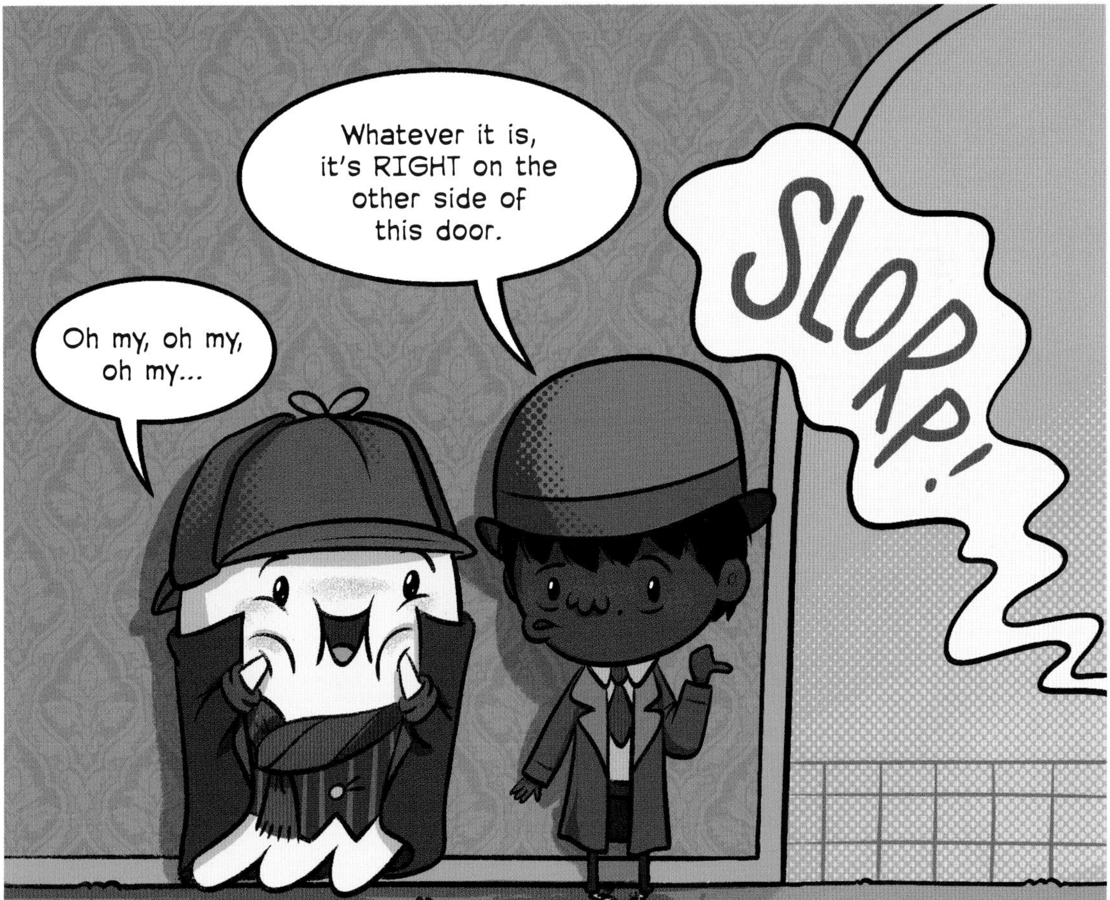
Whatever it is, it's RIGHT on the other side of this door.
Oh my, oh my, oh my...
SLORP!

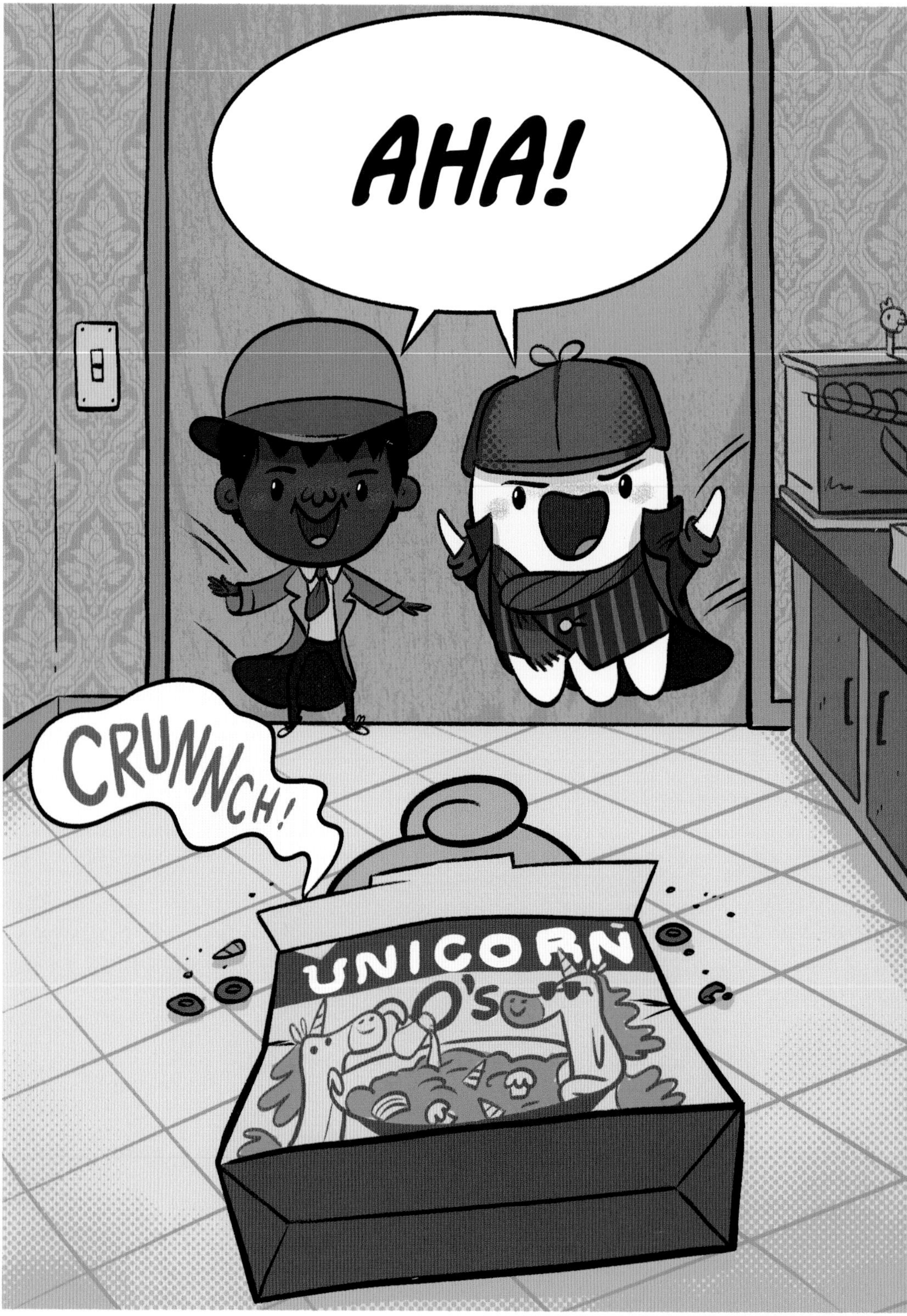
AHA!
CRUNNCH!
UNICORN O's

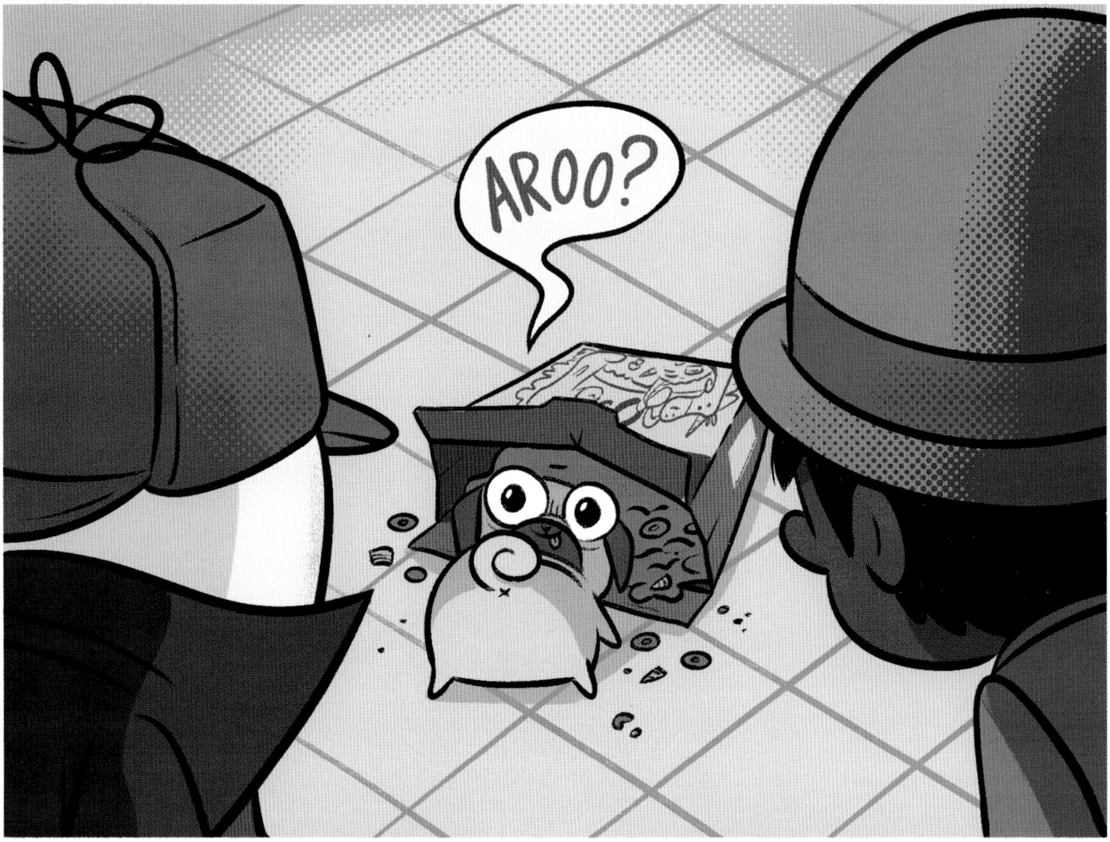
AROO?

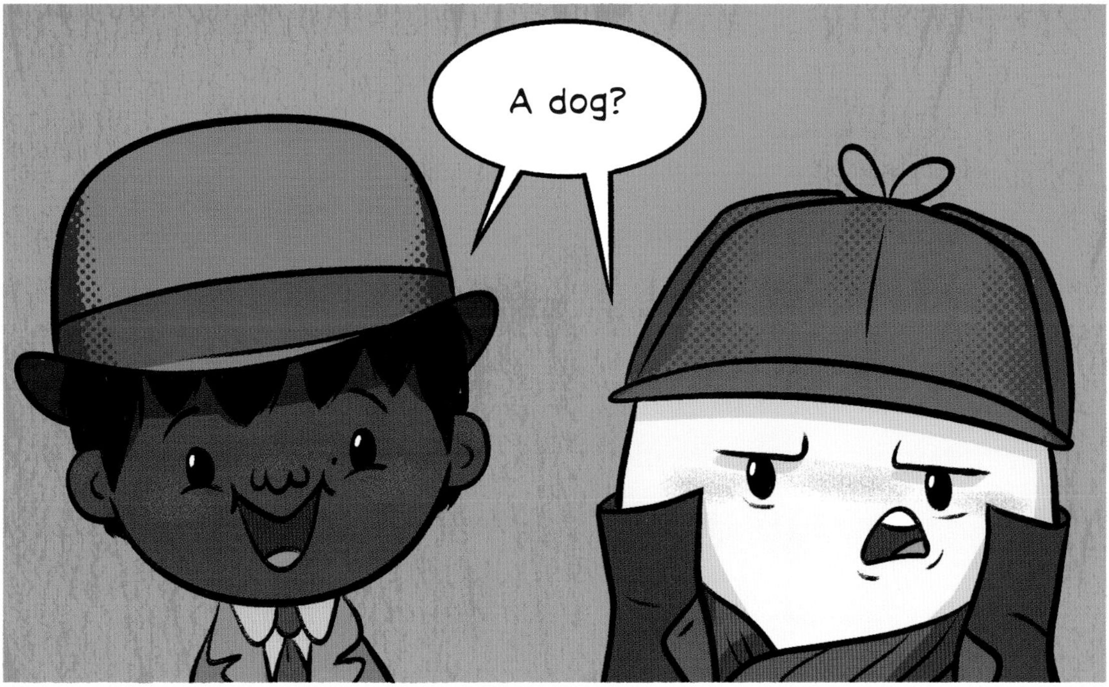
A dog?

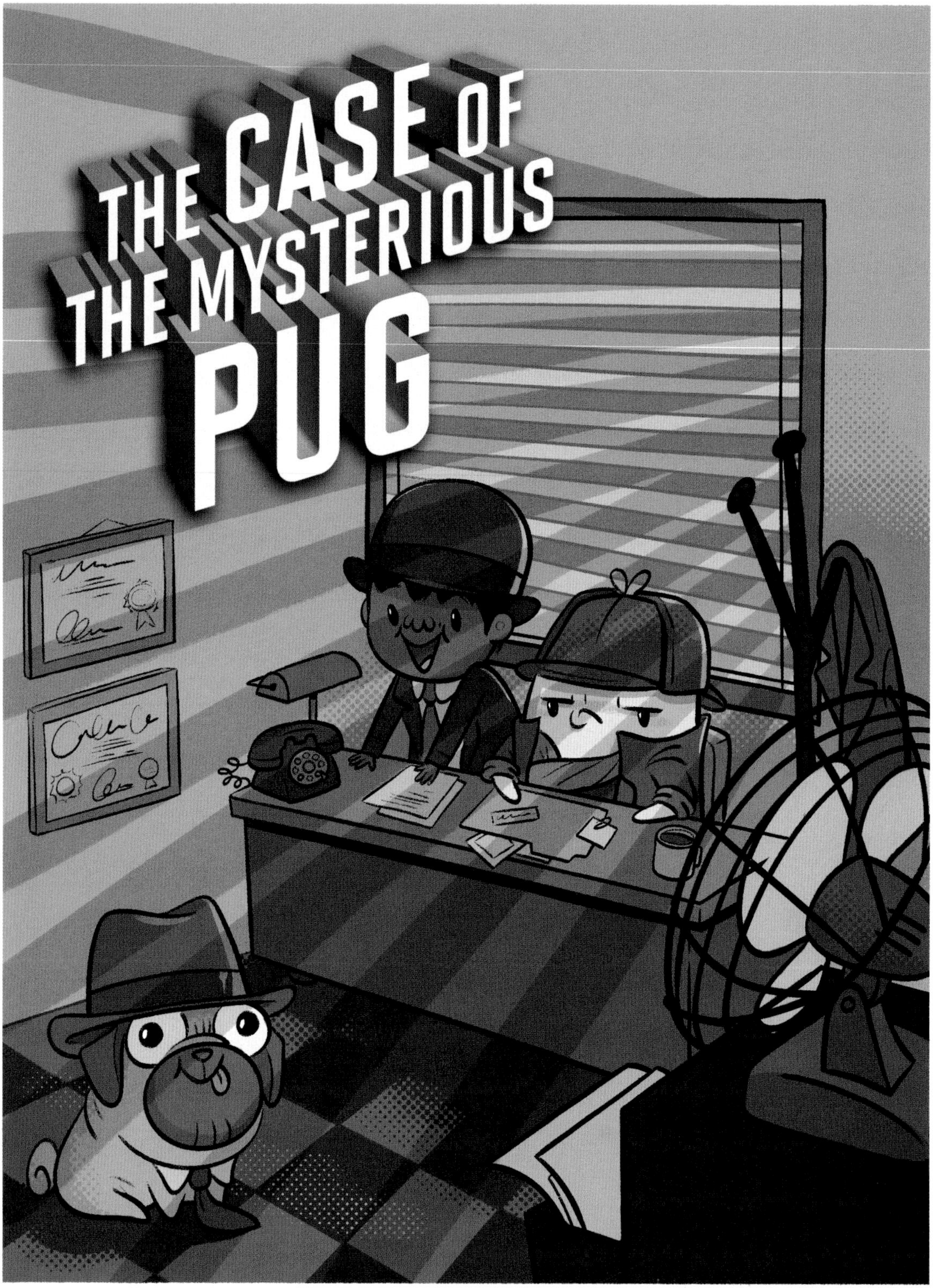
THE CASE OF
THE MYSTERIOUS
PUG

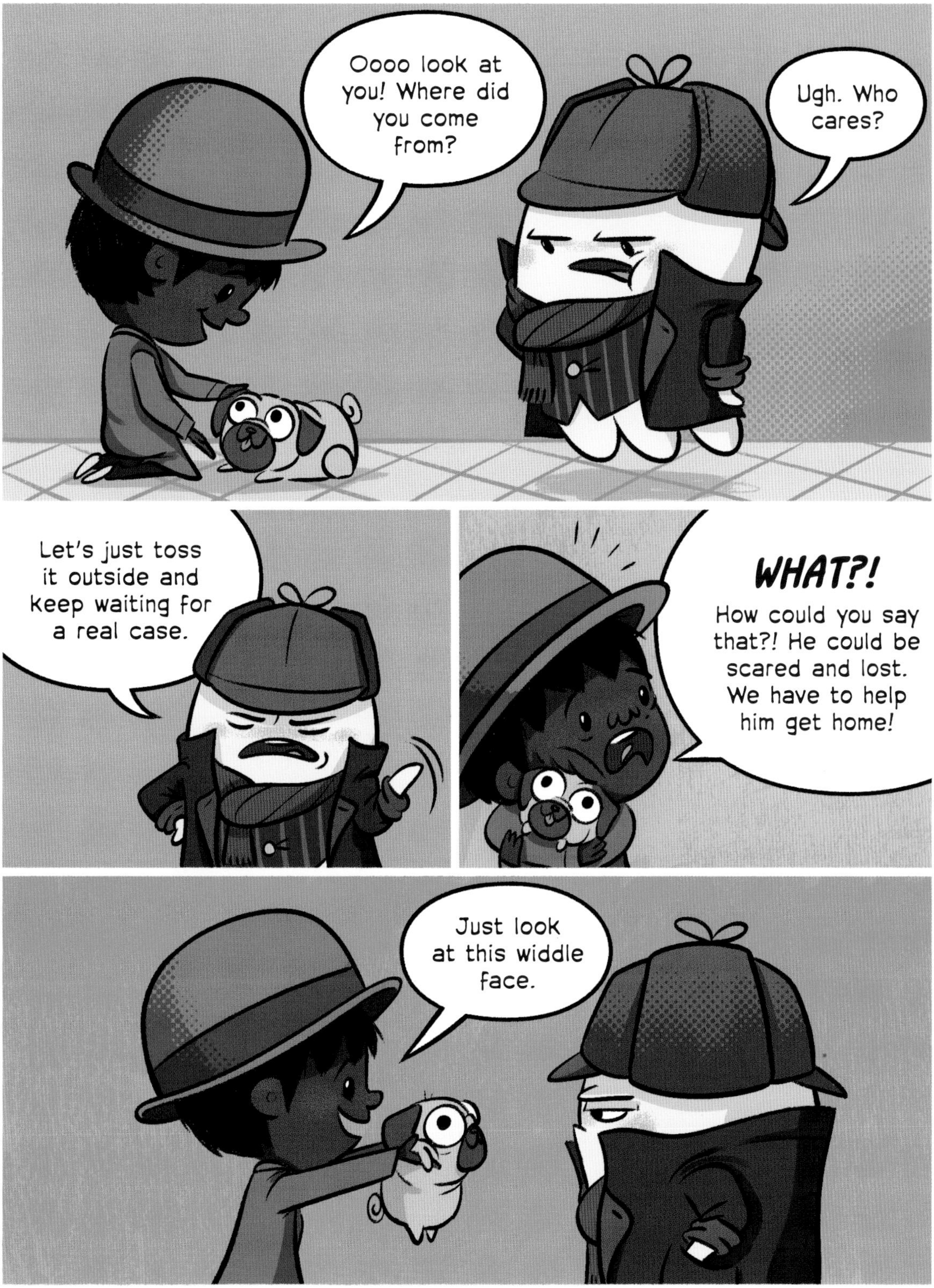
Oooo look at you! Where did you come from?
Ugh. Who cares?
Let's just toss it outside and keep waiting for a real case.
WHAT?!
How could you say that?! He could be scared and lost. We have to help him get home!
Just look at this widdle face.

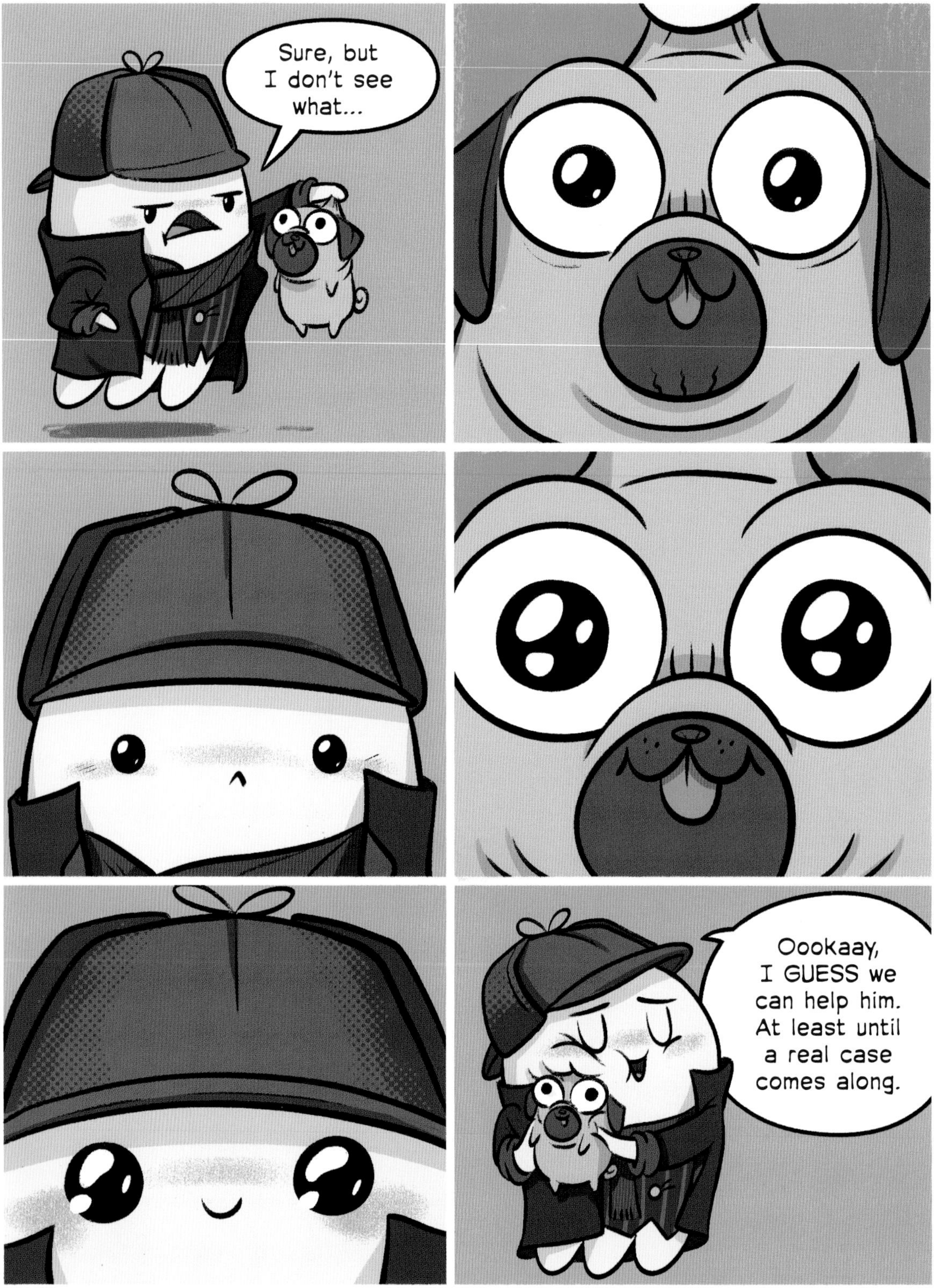
Sure, but I don't see what...
Oookaay, I GUESS we can help him. At least until a real case comes along.

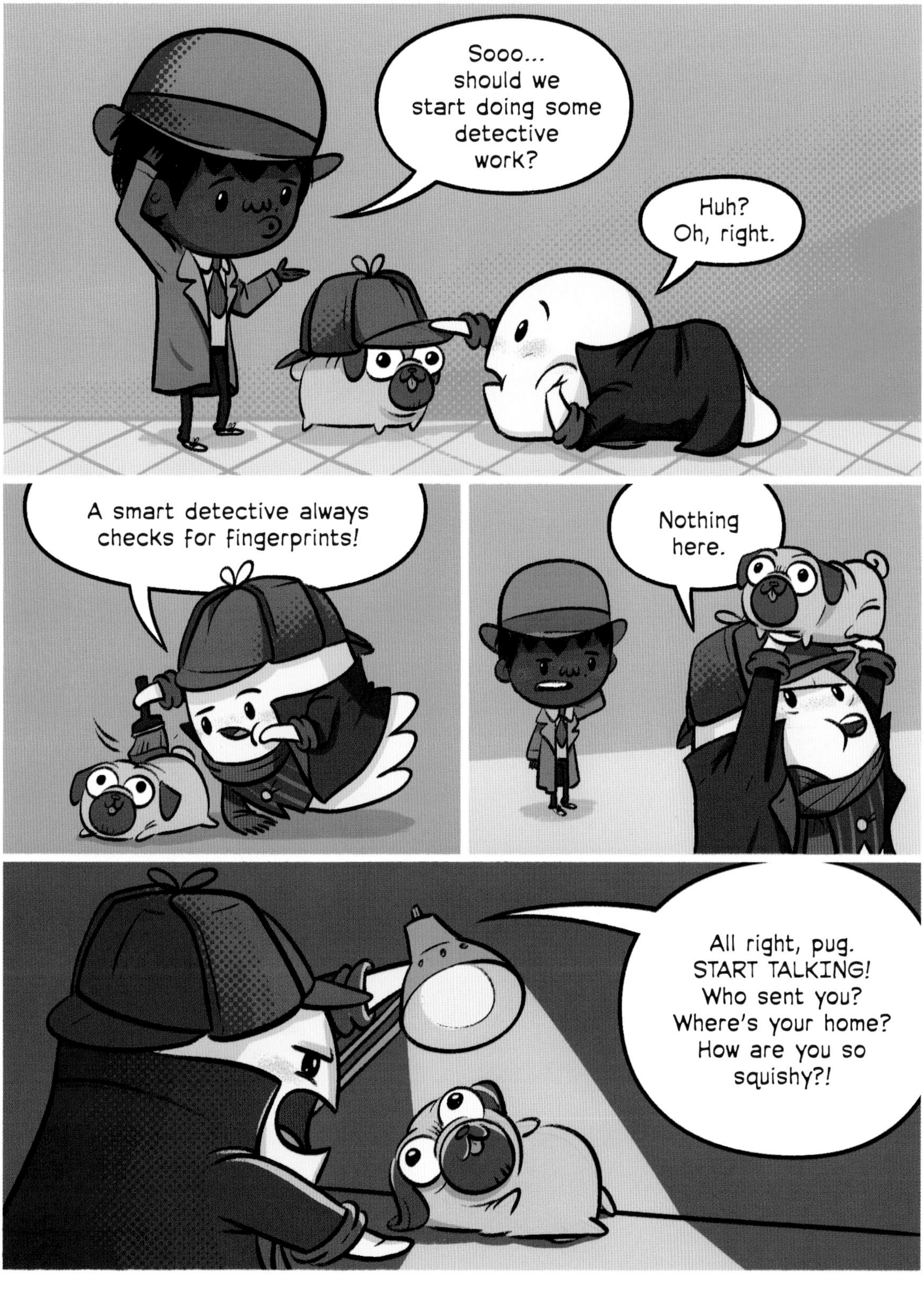
Sooo... should we start doing some detective work?
Huh? Oh, right.
A smart detective always checks for fingerprints!
Nothing here.
All right, pug. START TALKING! Who sent you? Where's your home? How are you so squishy?!

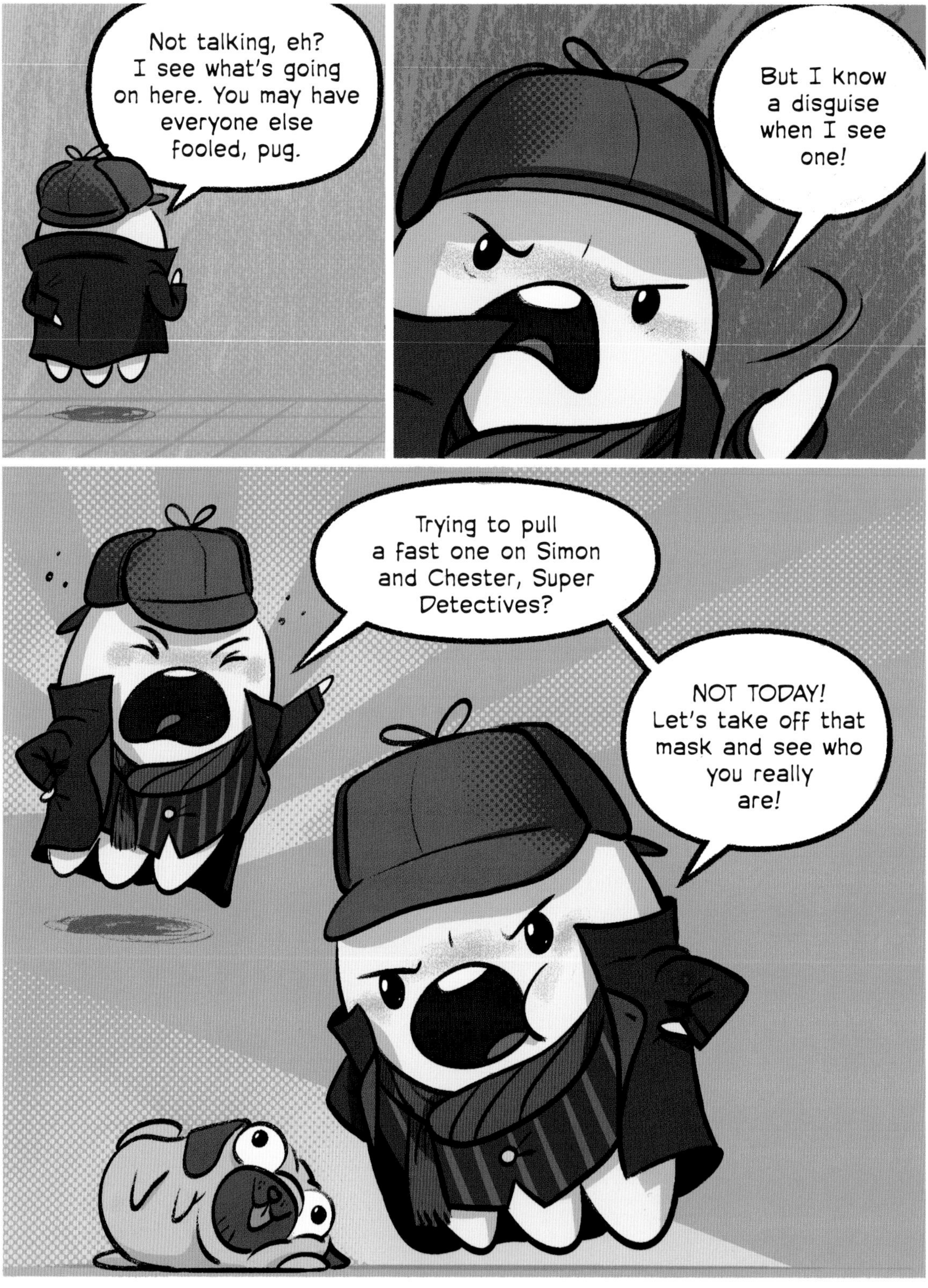
Not talking, eh? I see what's going on here. You may have everyone else fooled, pug.
But I know a disguise when I see one!
Trying to pull a fast one on Simon and Chester, Super Detectives?
NOT TODAY! Let's take off that mask and see who you really are!

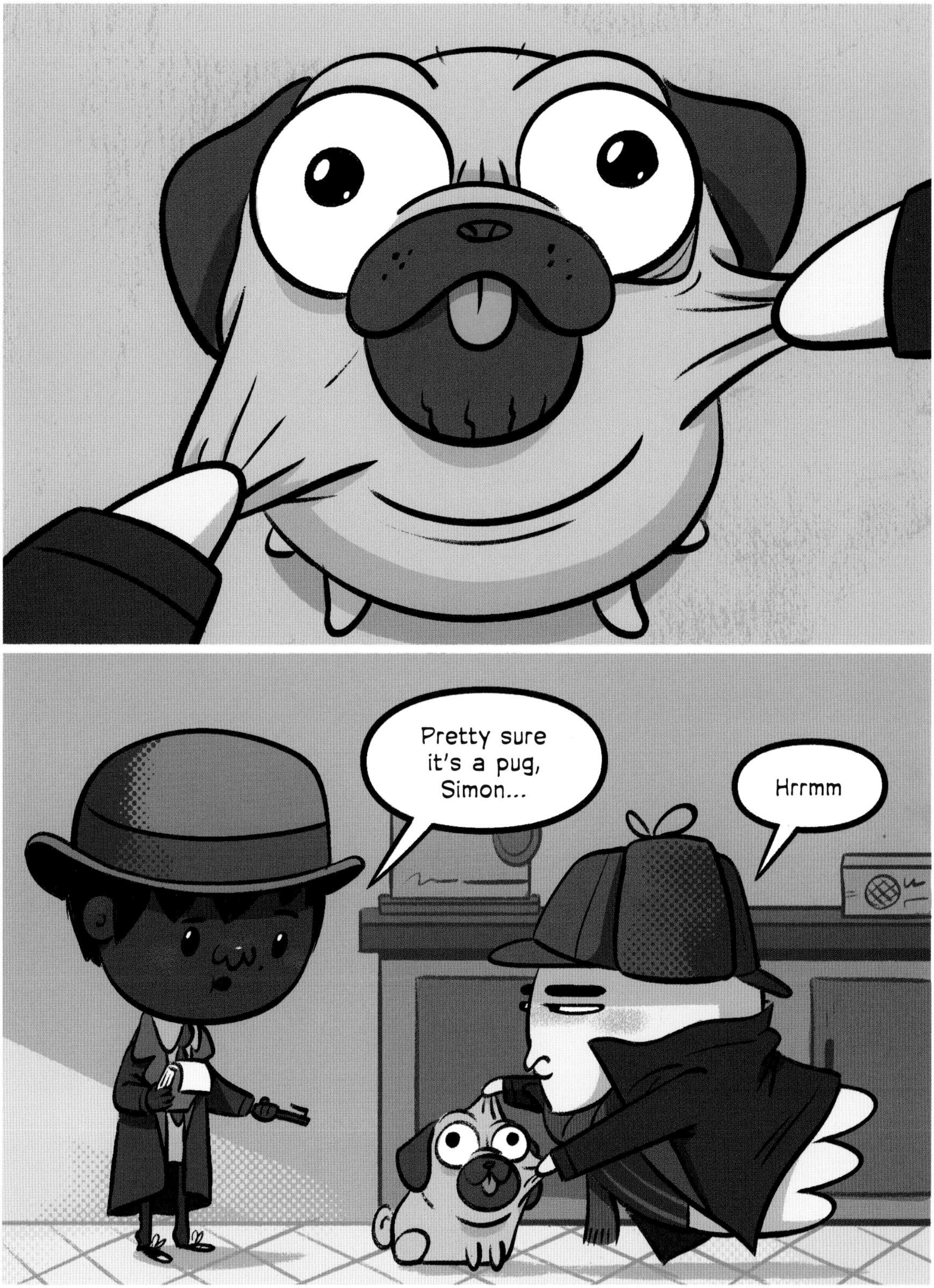
Pretty sure it's a pug, Simon...
Hrrmm

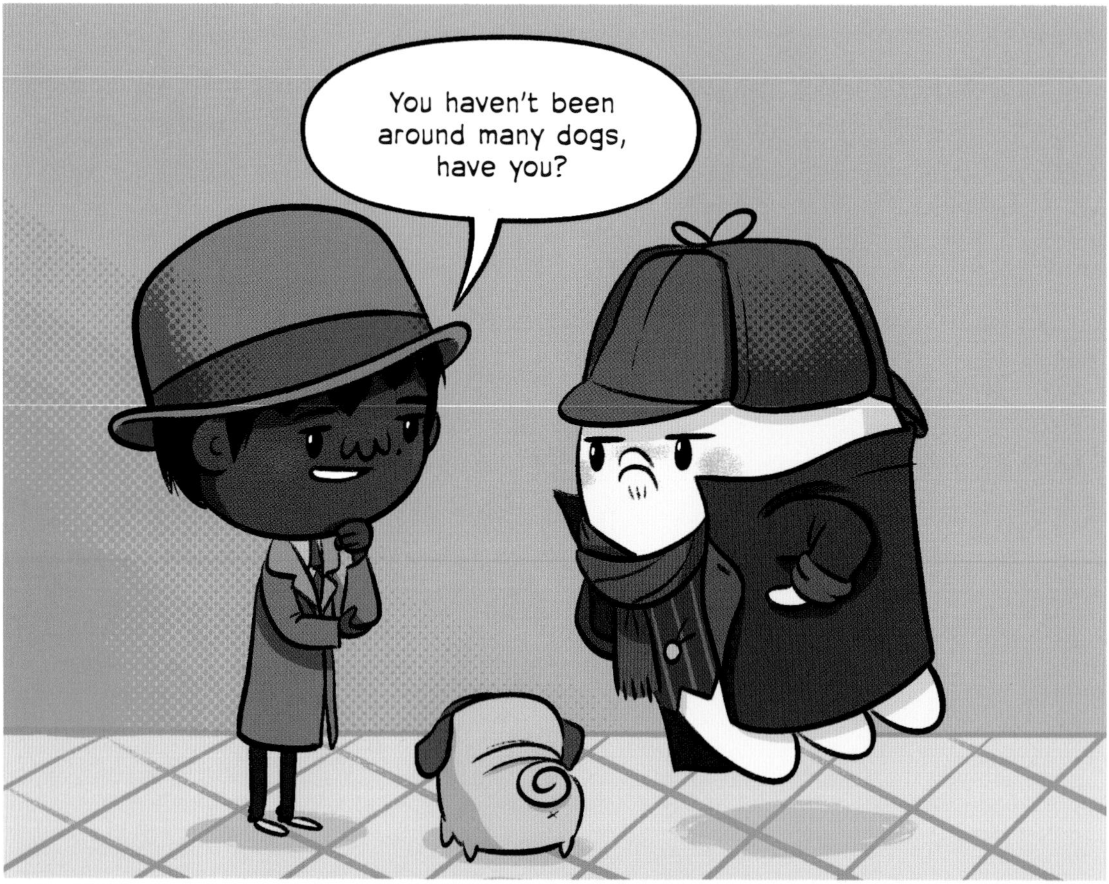
You haven't been around many dogs, have you?

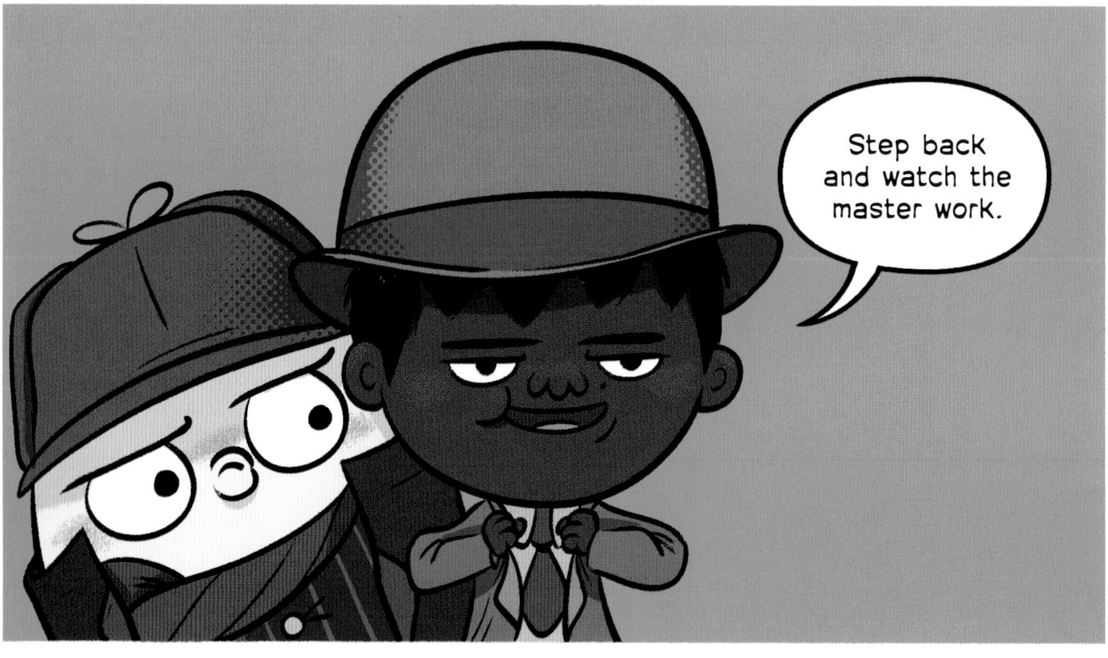
Step back and watch the master work.

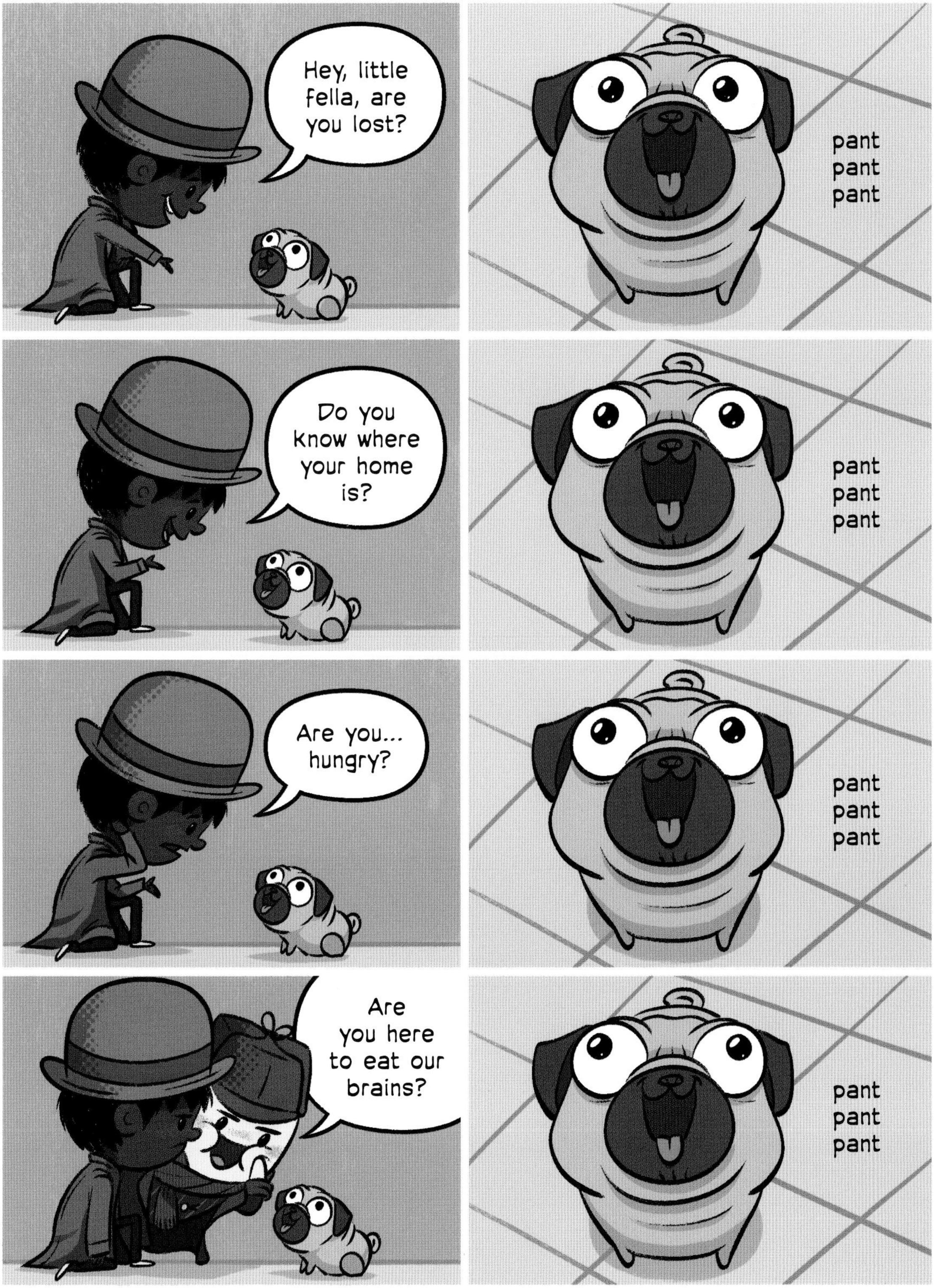
Hey, little fella, are you lost?
pant pant pant
Do you know where your home is?
pant pant pant
Are you... hungry?
pant pant pant
Are you here to eat our brains?
pant pant pant

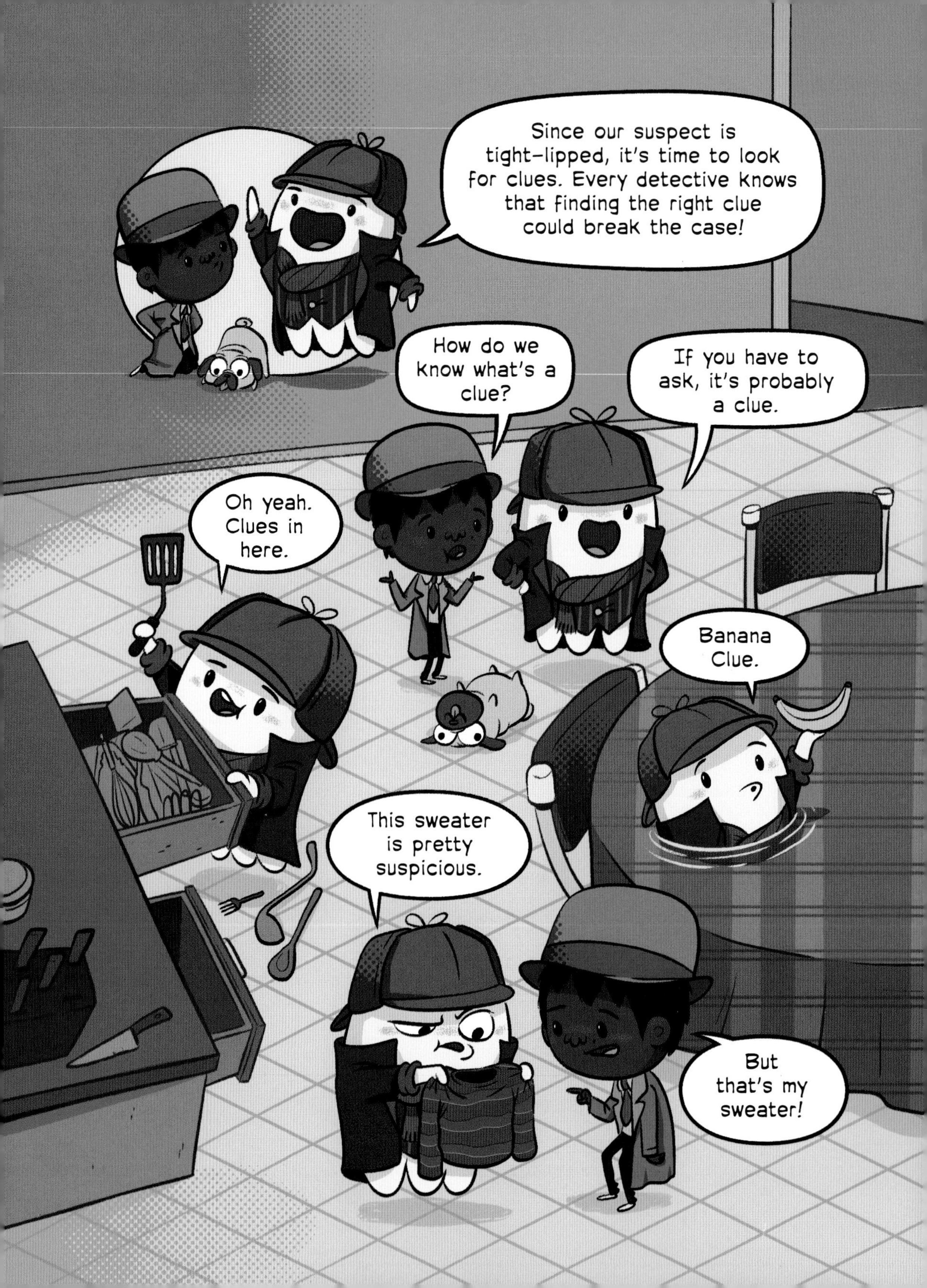
Since our suspect is tight-lipped, it's time to look for clues. Every detective knows that finding the right clue could break the case!
How do we know what's a clue?
If you have to ask, it's probably a clue.
Oh yeah. Clues in here.
Banana Clue.
This sweater is pretty suspicious.
But that's my sweater!

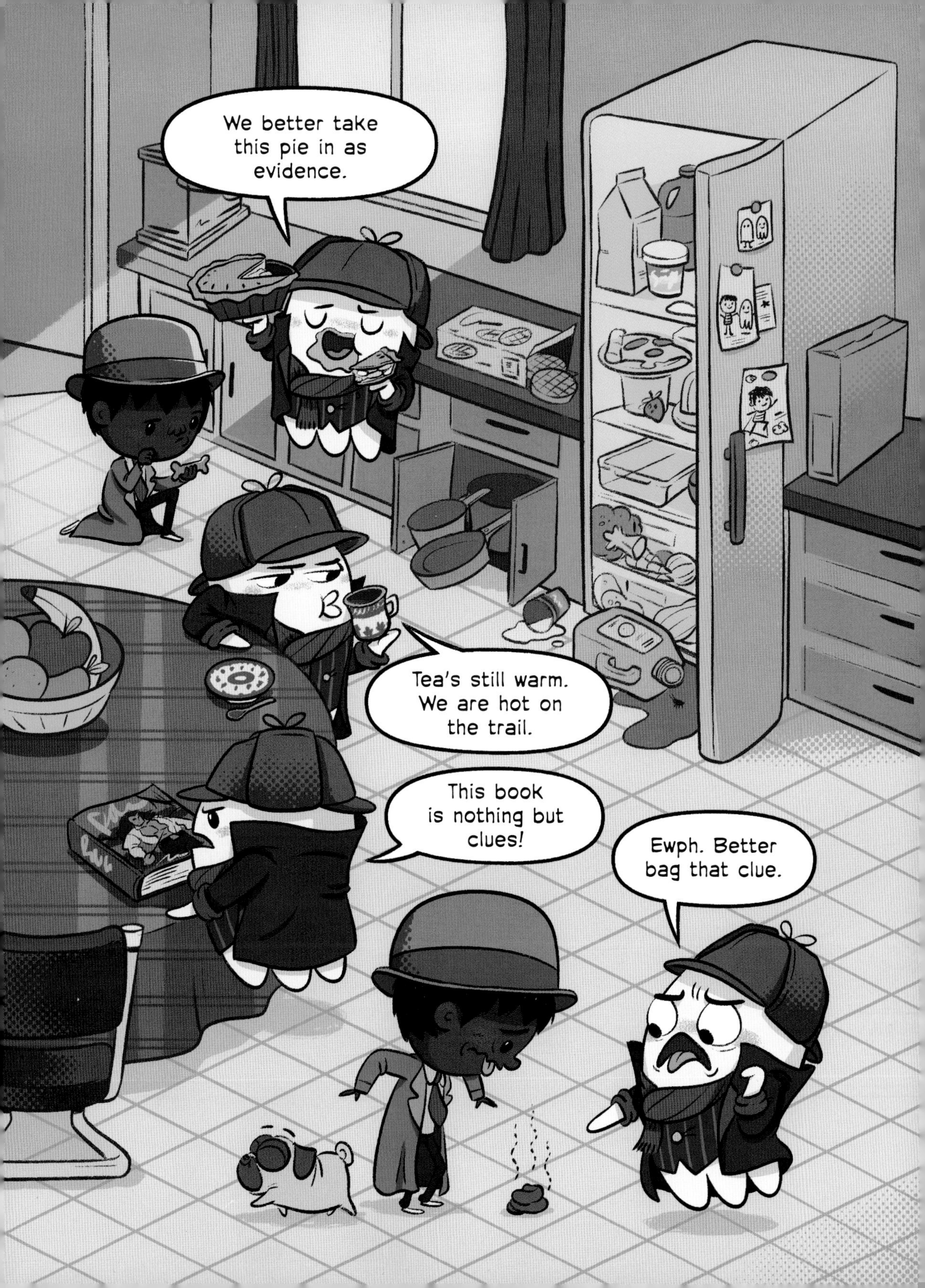
We better take this pie in as evidence.
Tea's still warm. We are hot on the trail.
This book is nothing but clues!
Ewph. Better bag that clue.

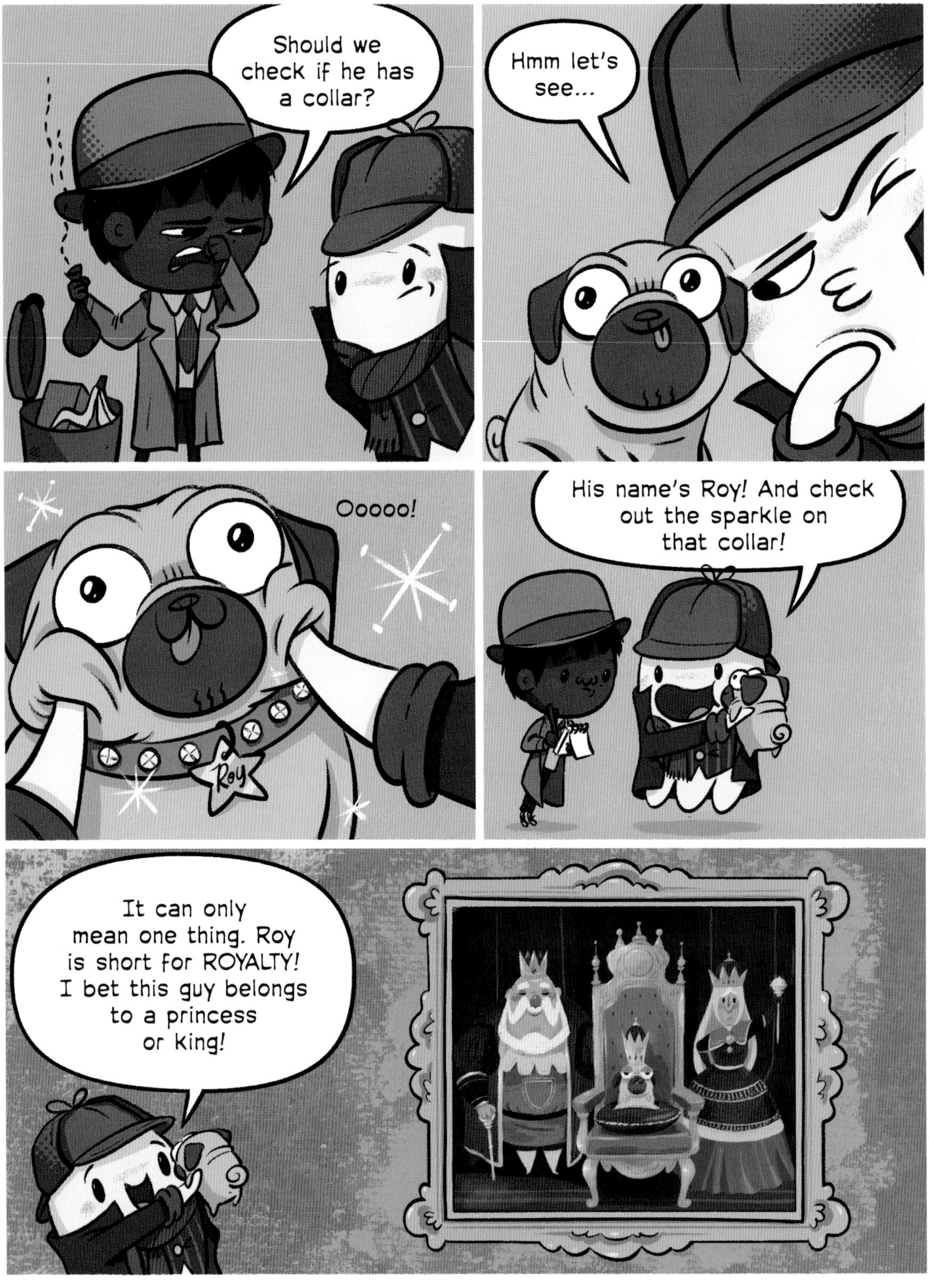
Should we check if he has a collar?
Hmm let's see...
Ooooo!
Roy
His name's Roy! And check out the sparkle on that collar!
It can only mean one thing. Roy is short for ROYALTY! I bet this guy belongs to a princess or king!

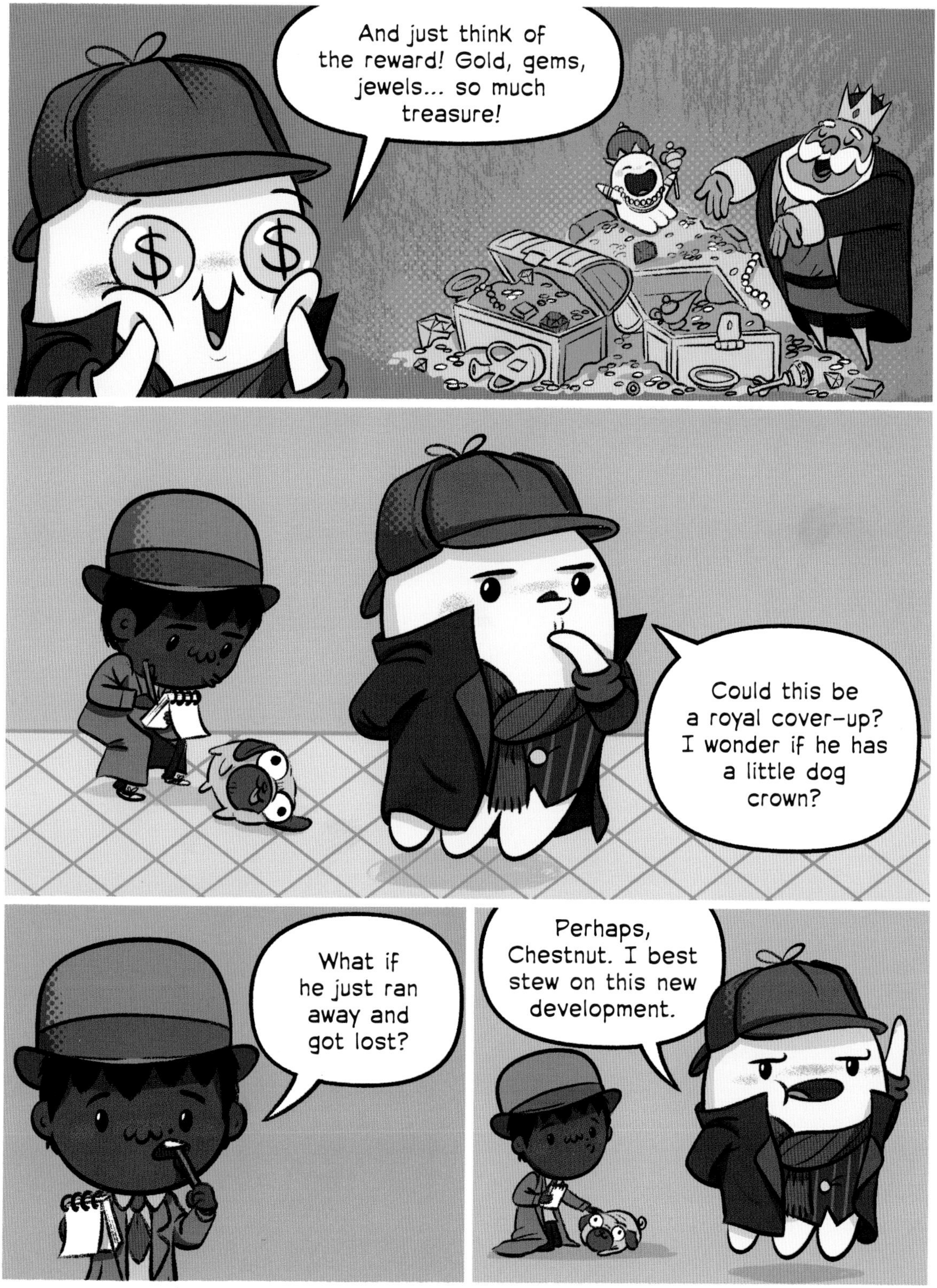

And just think of the reward! Gold, gems, jewels... so much treasure!
Could this be a royal cover-up? I wonder if he has a little dog crown?
What if he just ran away and got lost?
Perhaps, Chestnut. I best stew on this new development.

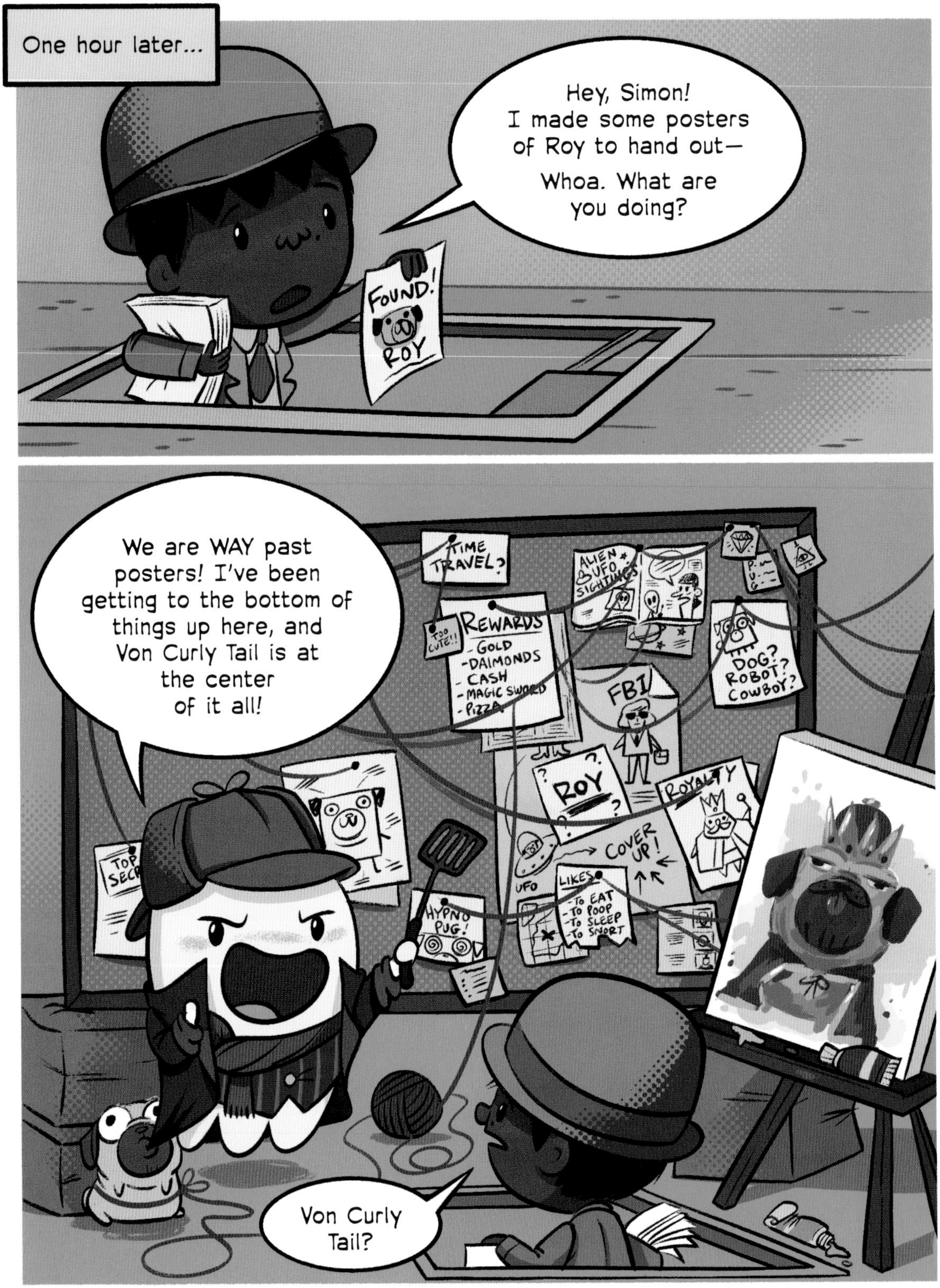
One hour later...
Hey, Simon! I made some posters of Roy to hand out—
Whoa. What are you doing?
FOUND! ROY
We are WAY past posters! I've been getting to the bottom of things up here, and Von Curly Tail is at the center of it all!
TIME TRAVEL?
TOO CUTE!!
REWARDS -GOLD -DAIMONDS -CASH -MAGIC SWORD -PIZZA
ALIEN UFO SIGHTINGS
DOG? ROBOT? COWBOY?
FBI
ROY
ROYALTY
COVER UP!
UFO
LIKES -To EAT -To POOP -To SLEEP -To SNORT
HYPNO PUG!
TOP SECR
Von Curly Tail?

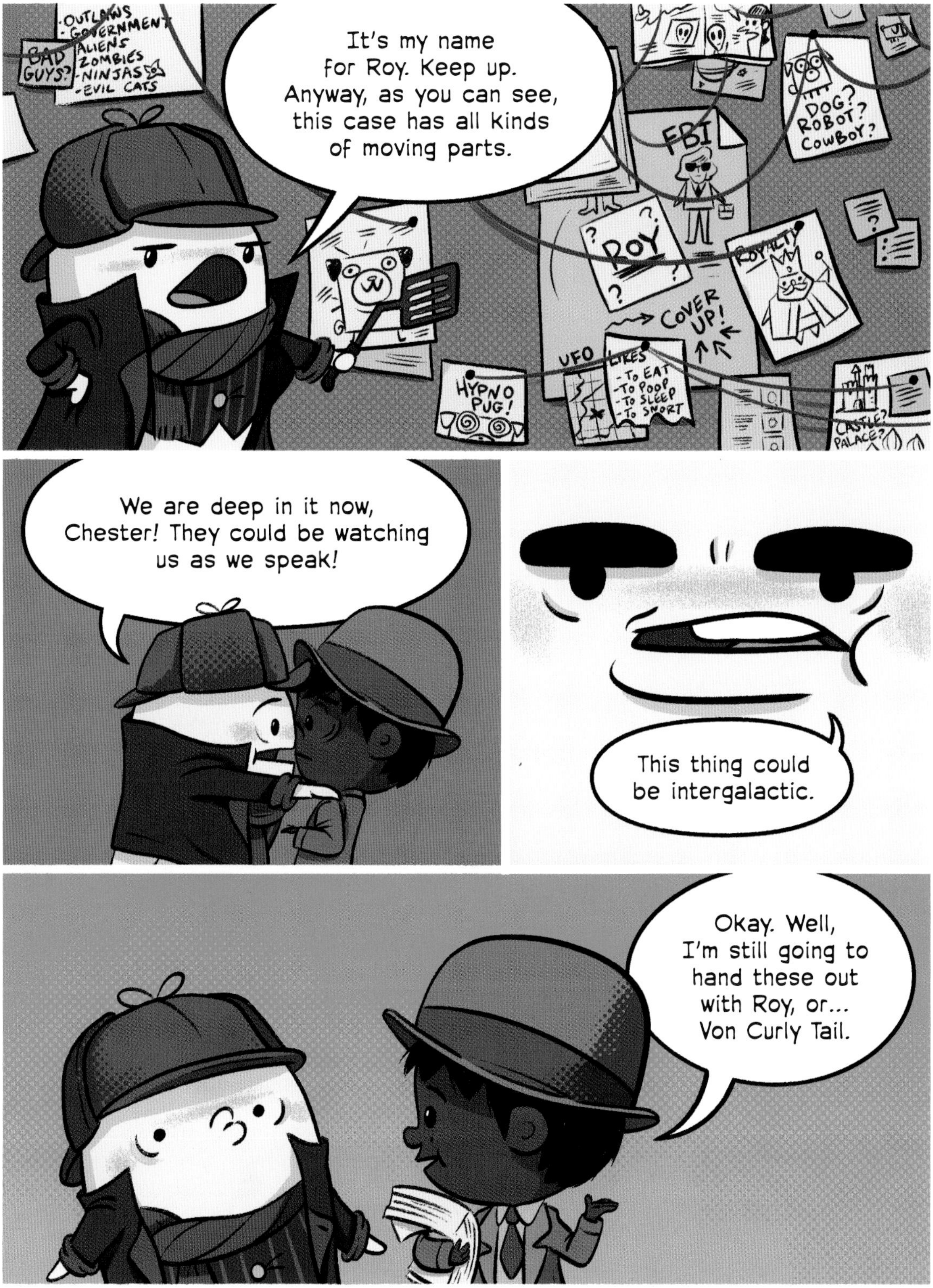
It's my name for Roy. Keep up. Anyway, as you can see, this case has all kinds of moving parts.
BAD GUYS?
-OUTLAWS
-GOVERNMENT
-ALIENS
-ZOMBIES
-NINJAS
-EVIL CATS
DOG? ROBOT? COWBOY?
FBI
ROY
ROYALTY
COVER UP!
UFO
HYPNO PUG!
LIKES -To EAT -To POOP -To SLEEP -To SNORT
CASTLE? PALACE?
We are deep in it now, Chester! They could be watching us as we speak!
This thing could be intergalactic.
Okay. Well, I'm still going to hand these out with Roy, or... Von Curly Tail.

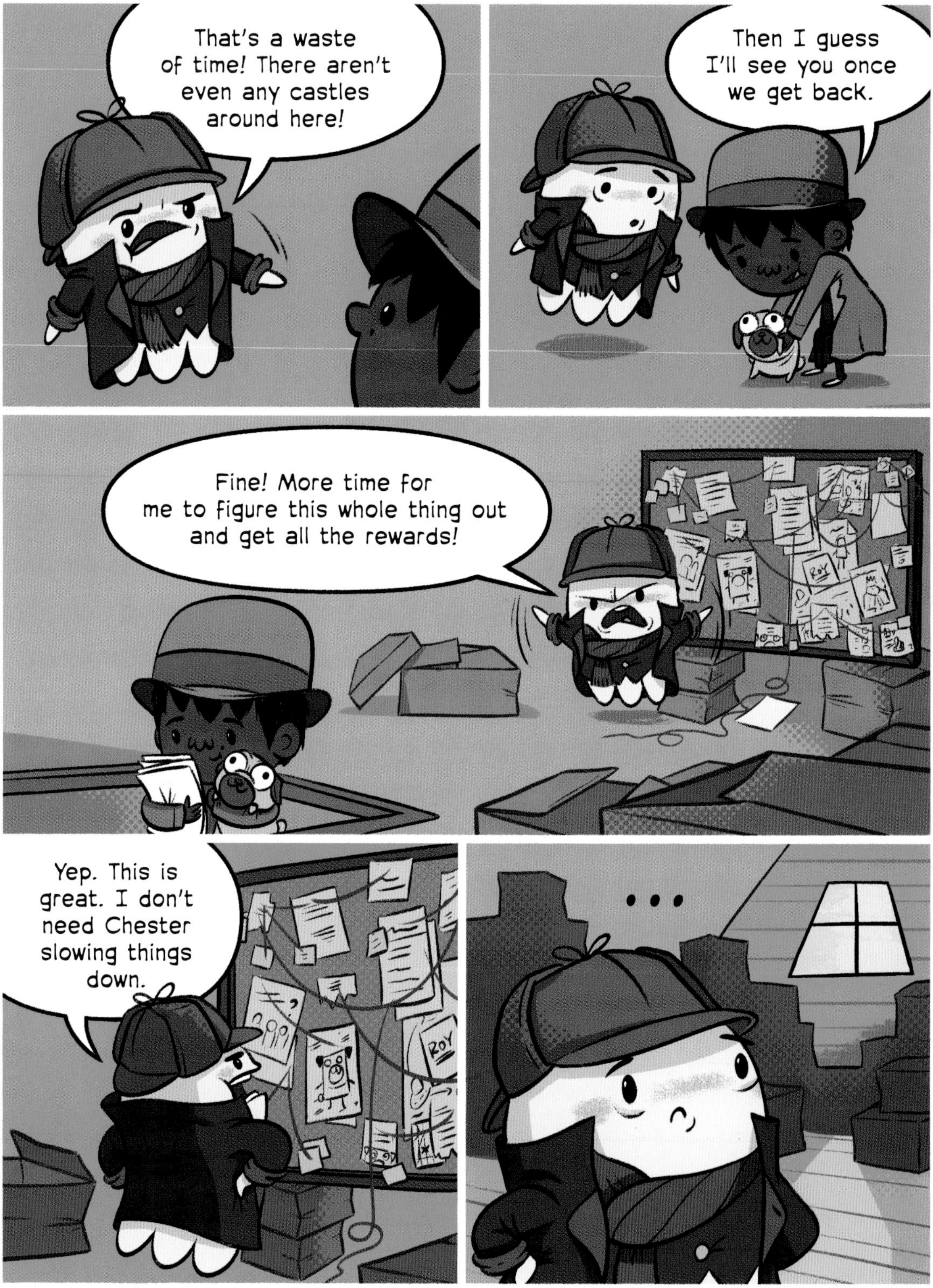
That's a waste of time! There aren't even any castles around here!
Then I guess I'll see you once we get back.
Fine! More time for me to figure this whole thing out and get all the rewards!
Yep. This is great. I don't need Chester slowing things down.
...

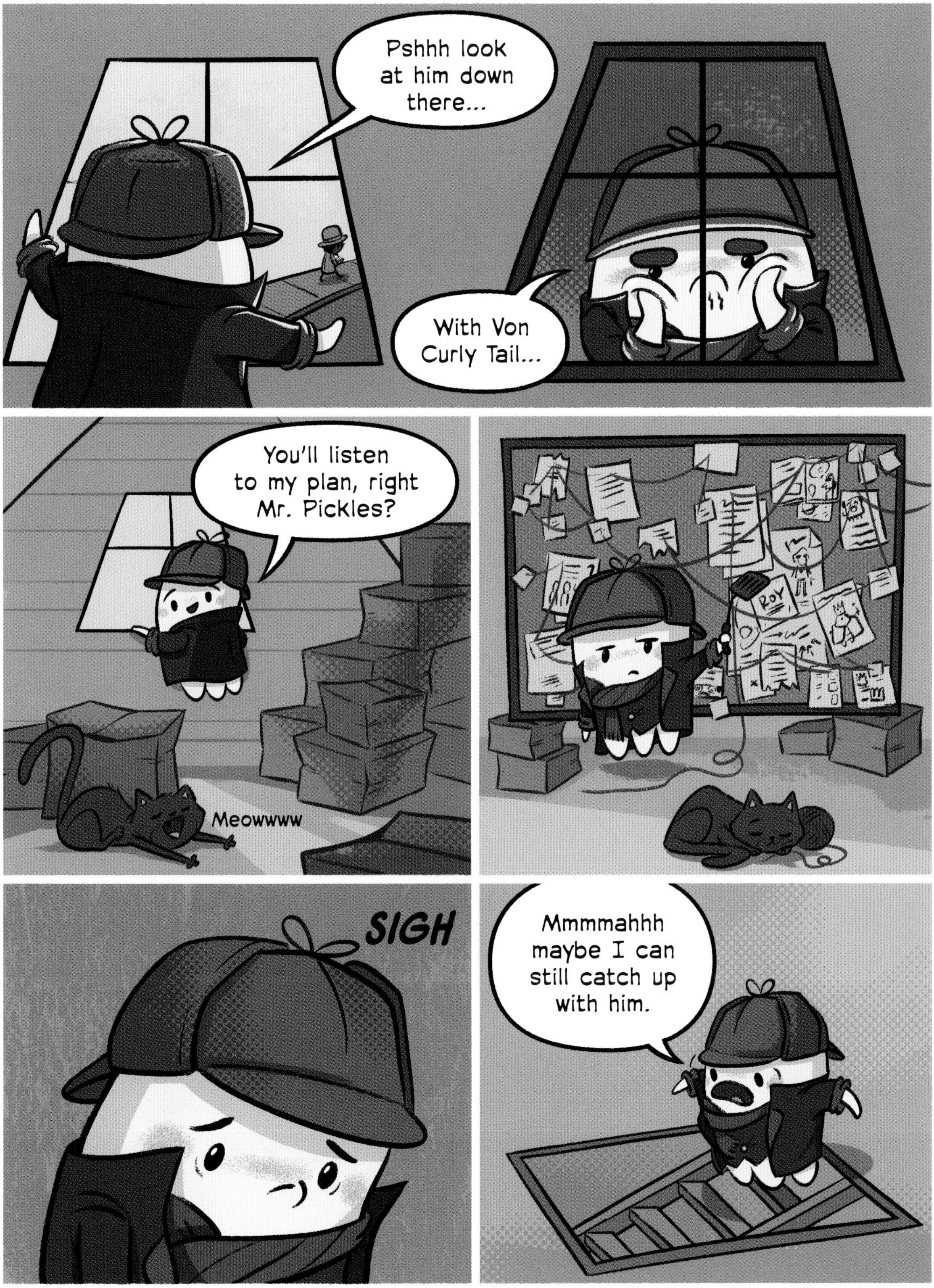
Pshhh look at him down there...
With Von Curly Tail...
You'll listen to my plan, right Mr. Pickles?
Meowwww
SIGH
Mmmmahhh maybe I can still catch up with him.

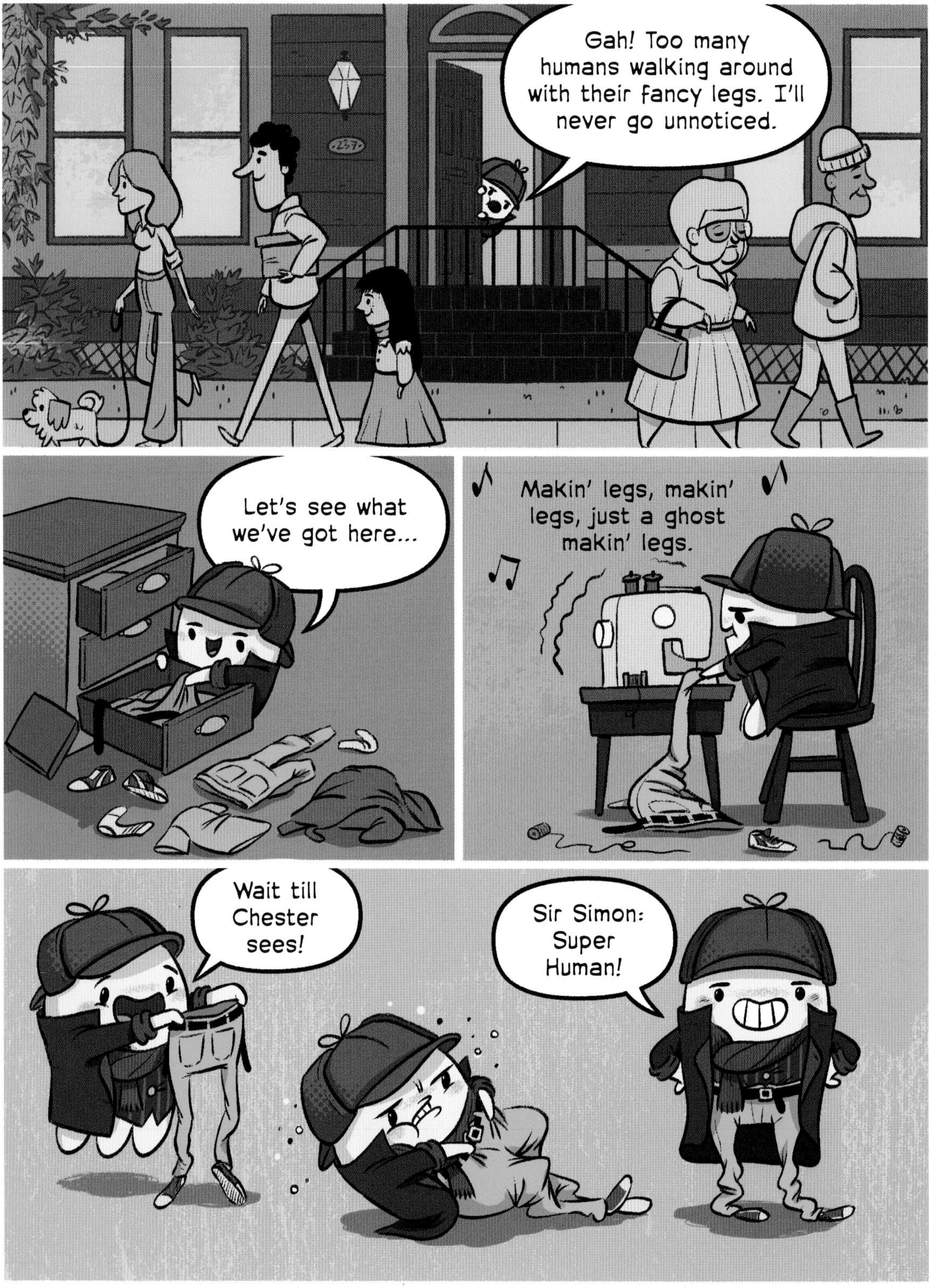
Gah! Too many humans walking around with their fancy legs. I'll never go unnoticed.
Let's see what we've got here...
Makin' legs, makin' legs, just a ghost makin' legs.
Wait till Chester sees!
Sir Simon: Super Human!

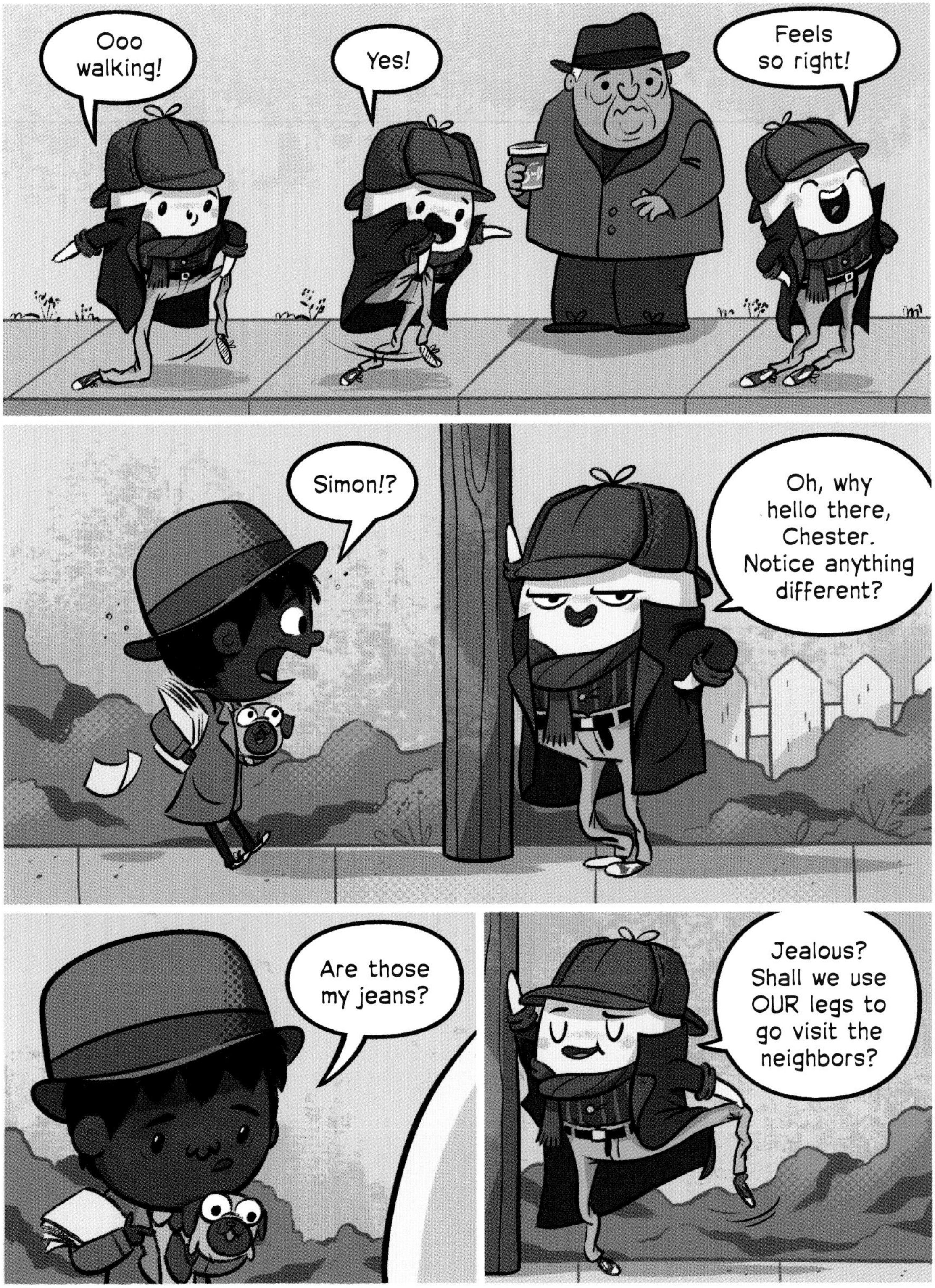
Ooo walking!
Yes!
Feels so right!
Simon!?
Oh, why hello there, Chester. Notice anything different?
Are those my jeans?
Jealous? Shall we use OUR legs to go visit the neighbors?

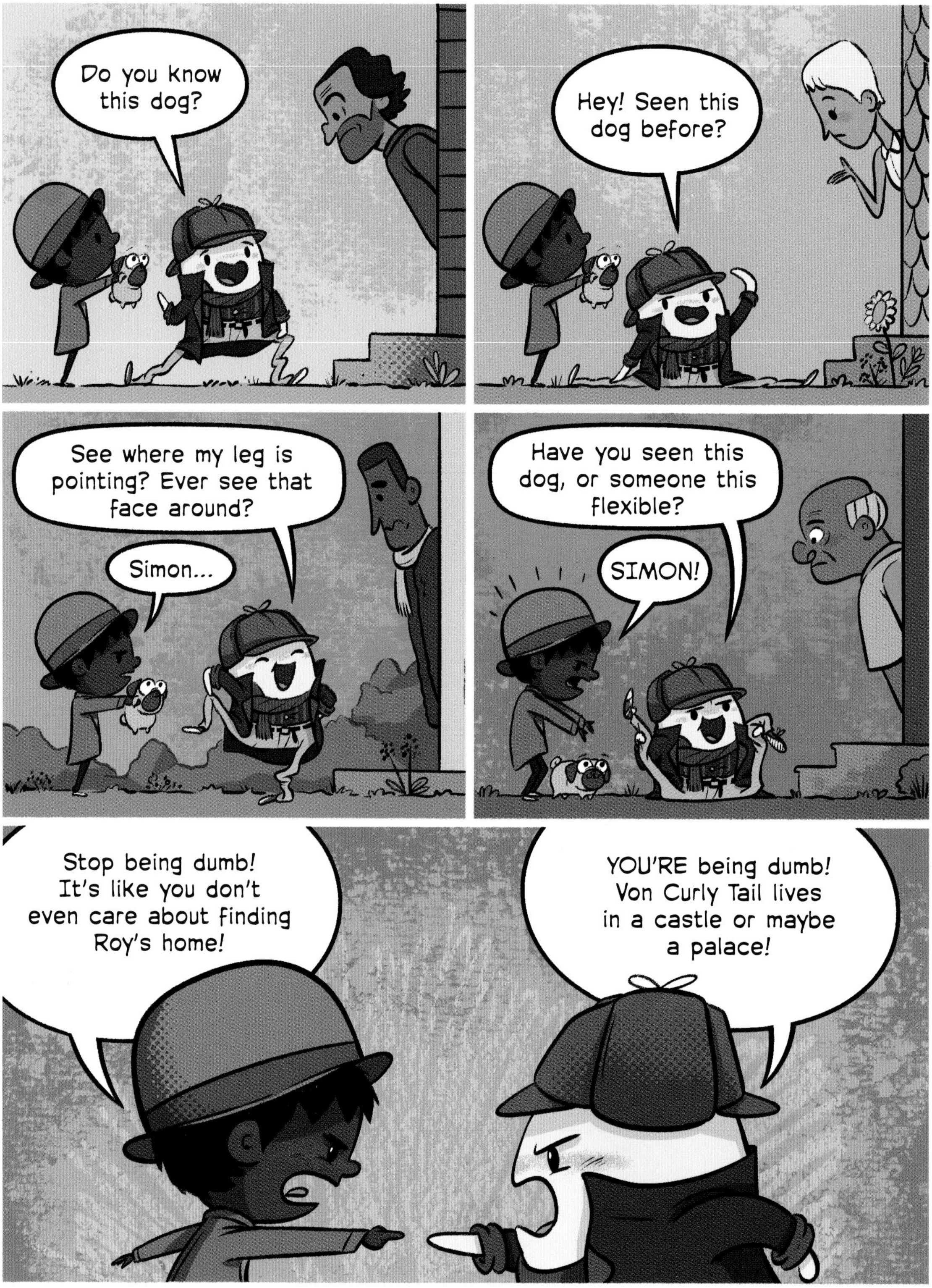
Do you know this dog?
Hey! Seen this dog before?
See where my leg is pointing? Ever see that face around?
Simon...
Have you seen this dog, or someone this flexible?
SIMON!
Stop being dumb! It's like you don't even care about finding Roy's home!
YOU'RE being dumb! Von Curly Tail lives in a castle or maybe a palace!

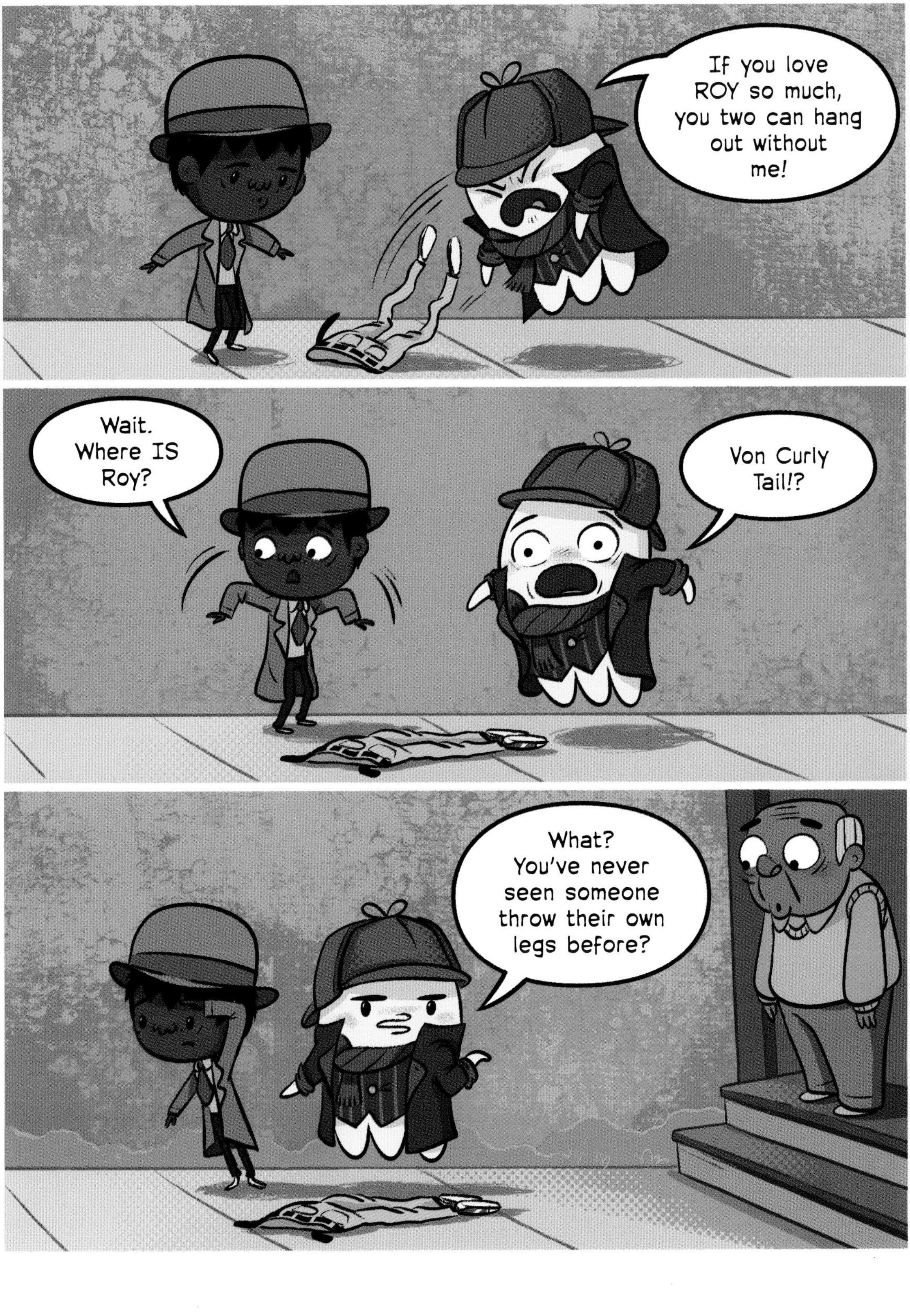
If you love ROY so much, you two can hang out without me!
Wait. Where IS Roy?
Von Curly Tail!?
What? You've never seen someone throw their own legs before?

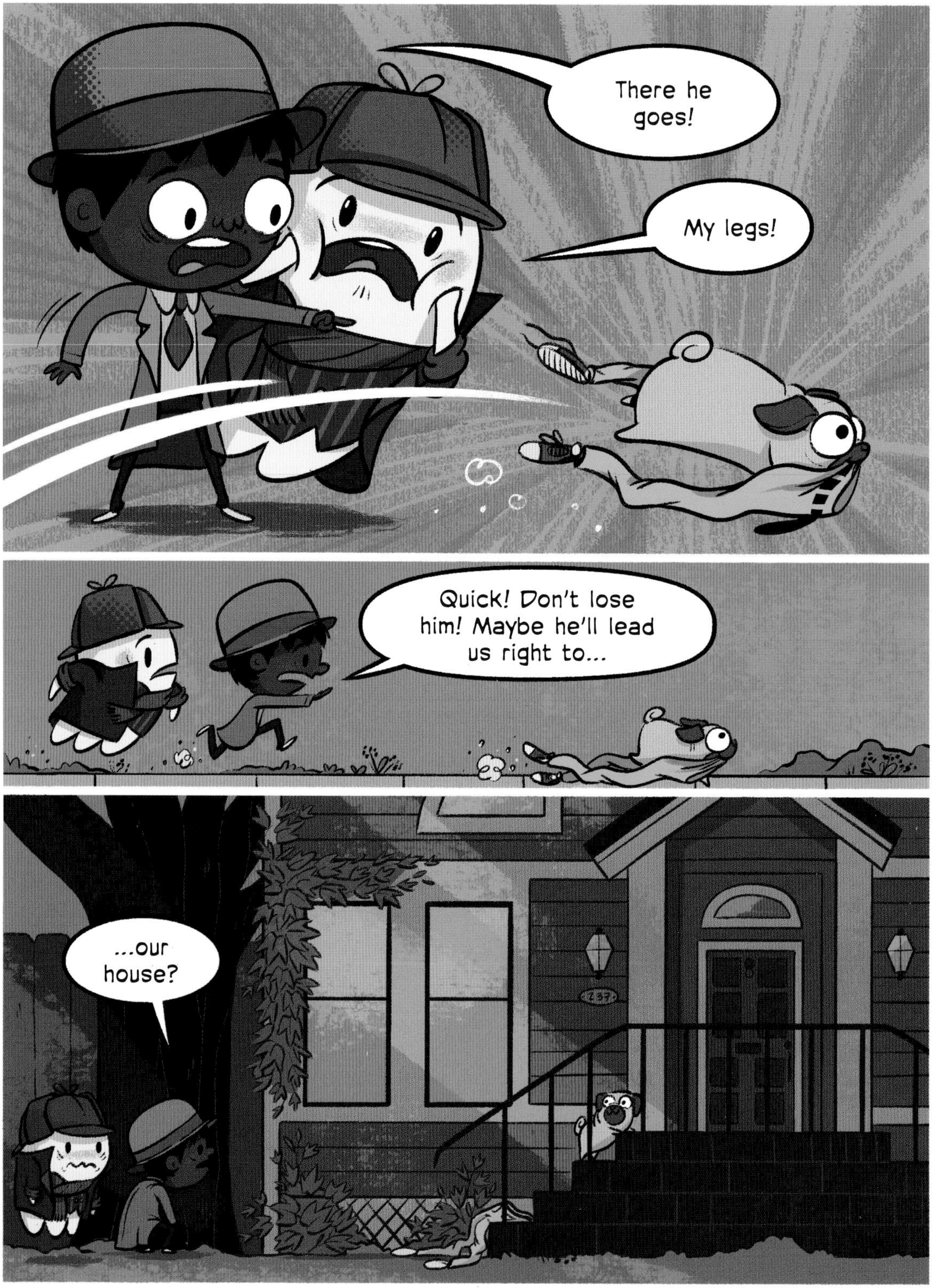
There he goes!
My legs!
Quick! Don't lose him! Maybe he'll lead us right to...
...our house?

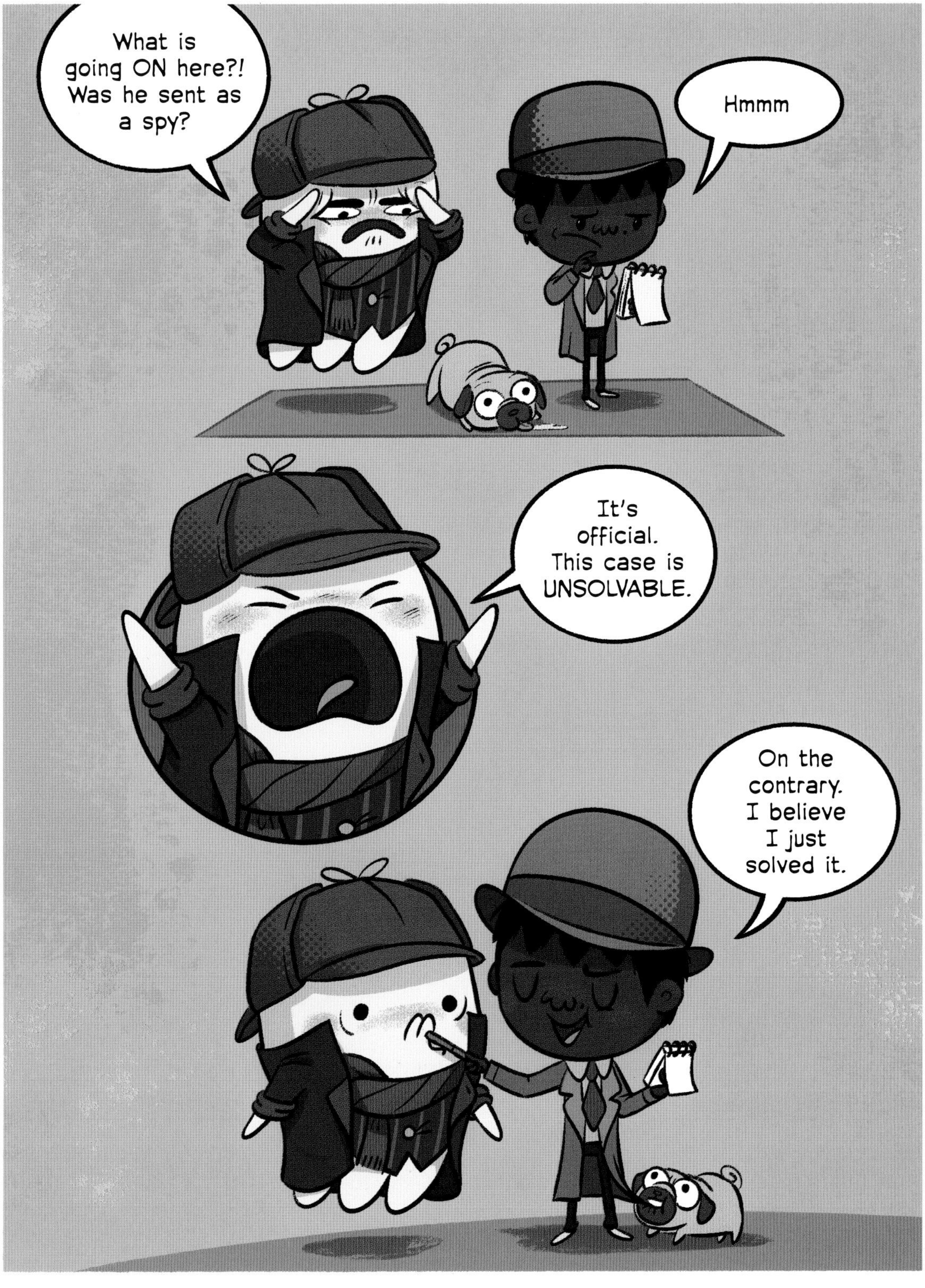
What is going ON here?! Was he sent as a spy?
Hmmm
It's official. This case is UNSOLVABLE.
On the contrary. I believe I just solved it.

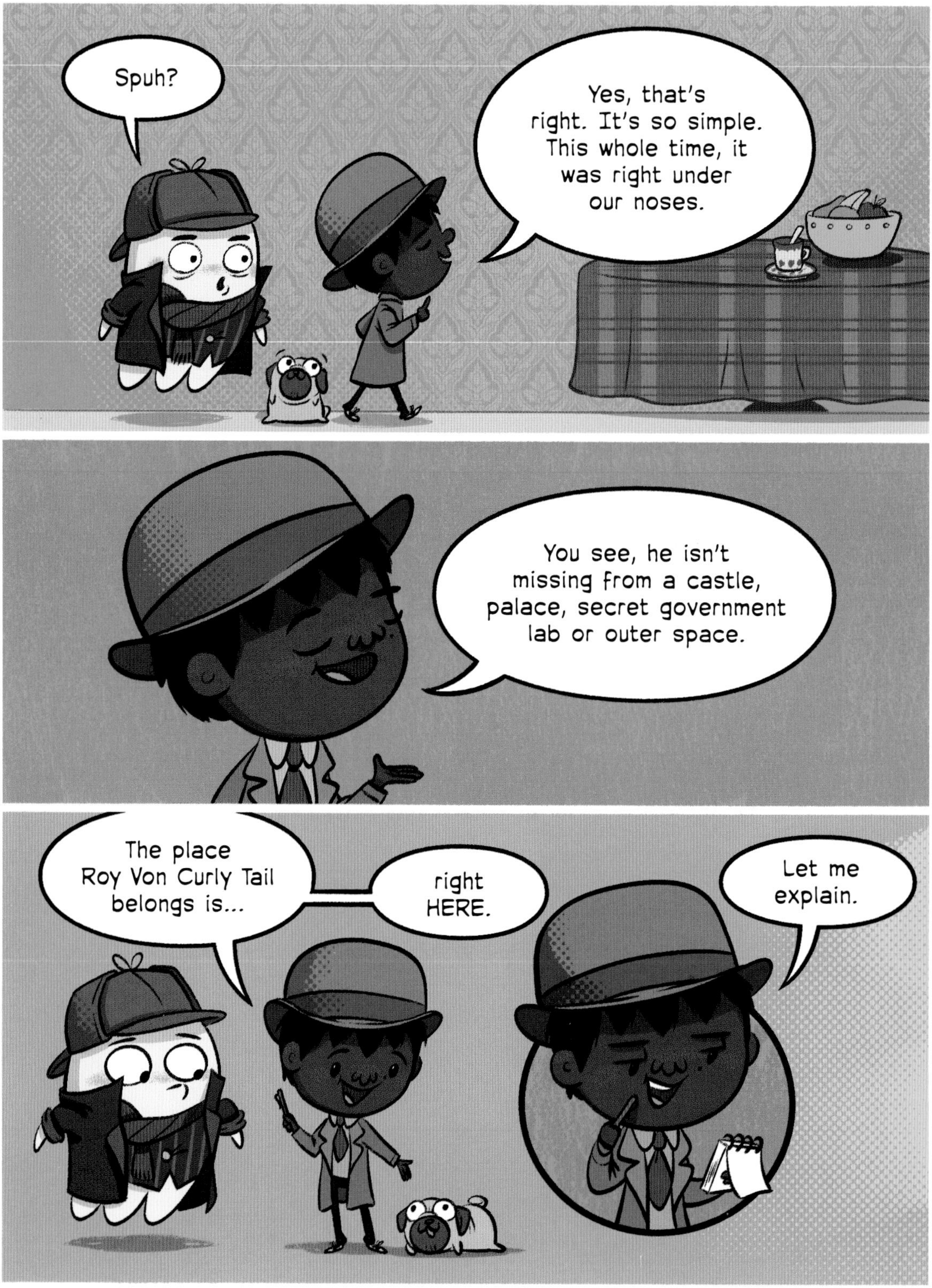
Spuh?
Yes, that's right. It's so simple. This whole time, it was right under our noses.
You see, he isn't missing from a castle, palace, secret government lab or outer space.
The place Roy Von Curly Tail belongs is...
right HERE.
Let me explain.

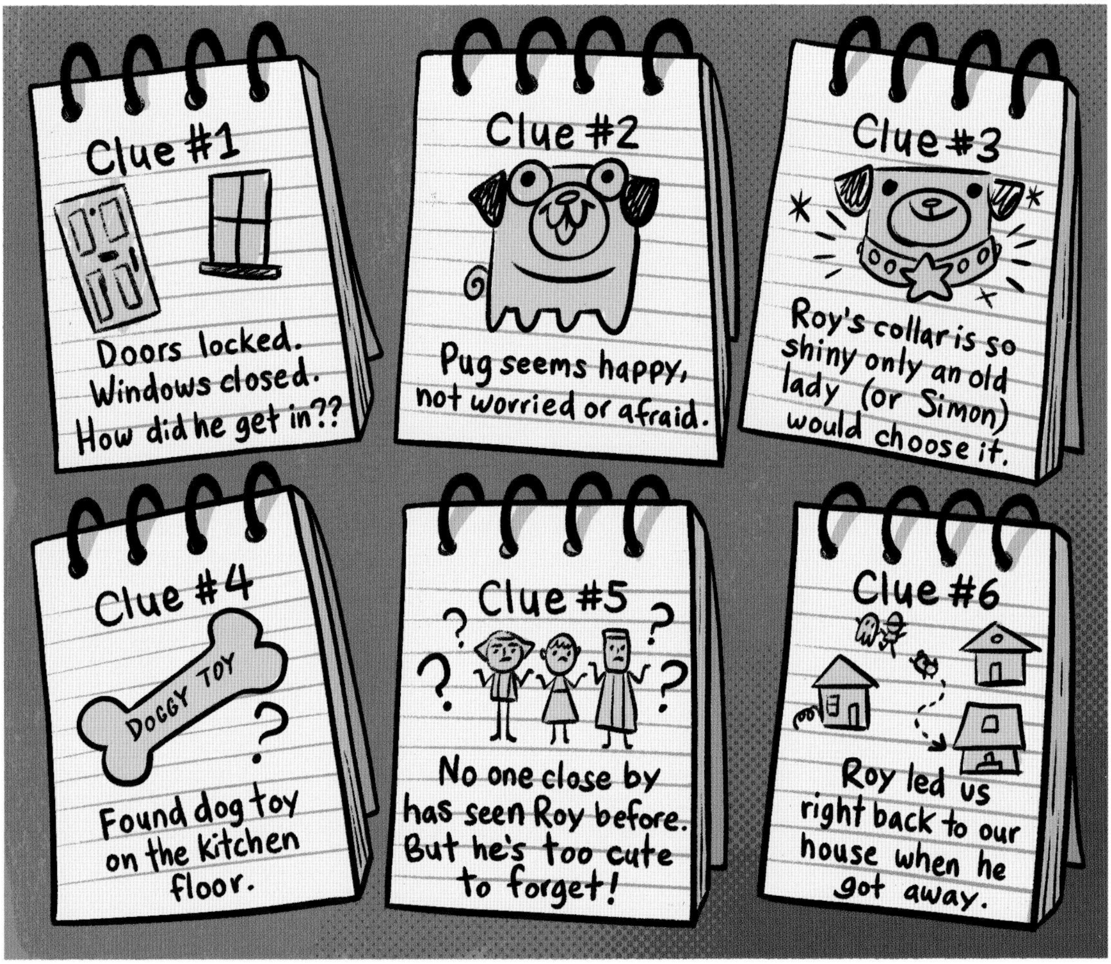
Clue #1
Doors locked. Windows closed. How did he get in??
Clue #2
Pug seems happy, not worried or afraid.
Clue #3
Roy's collar is so shiny only an old lady (or Simon) would choose it.
Clue #4
DOGGY TOY
Found dog toy on the kitchen floor.
Clue #5
No one close by has seen Roy before. But he's too cute to forget!
Clue #6
Roy led us right back to our house when he got away.

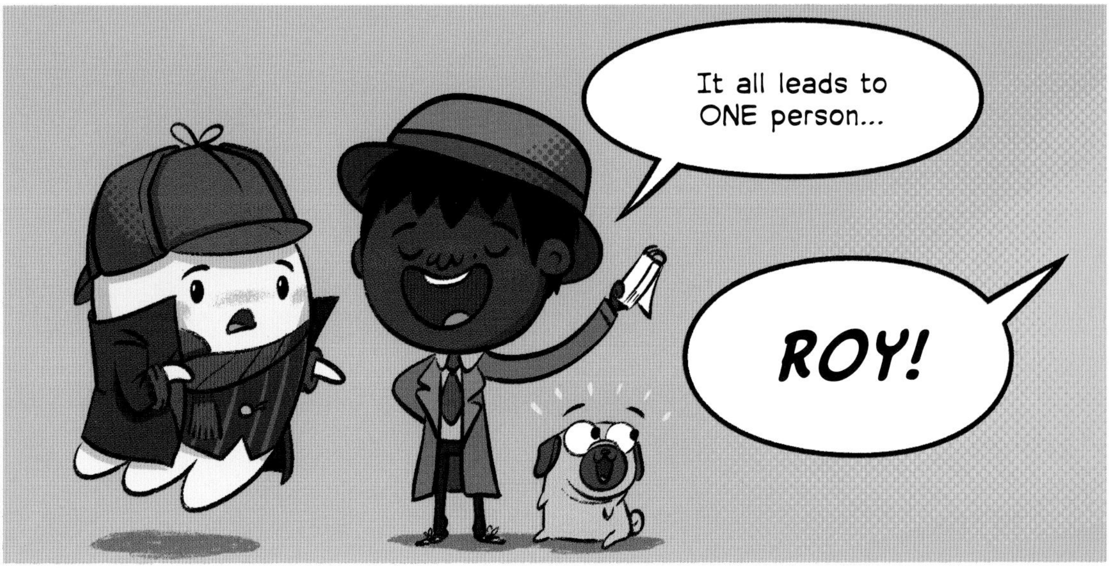
It all leads to ONE person...
ROY!

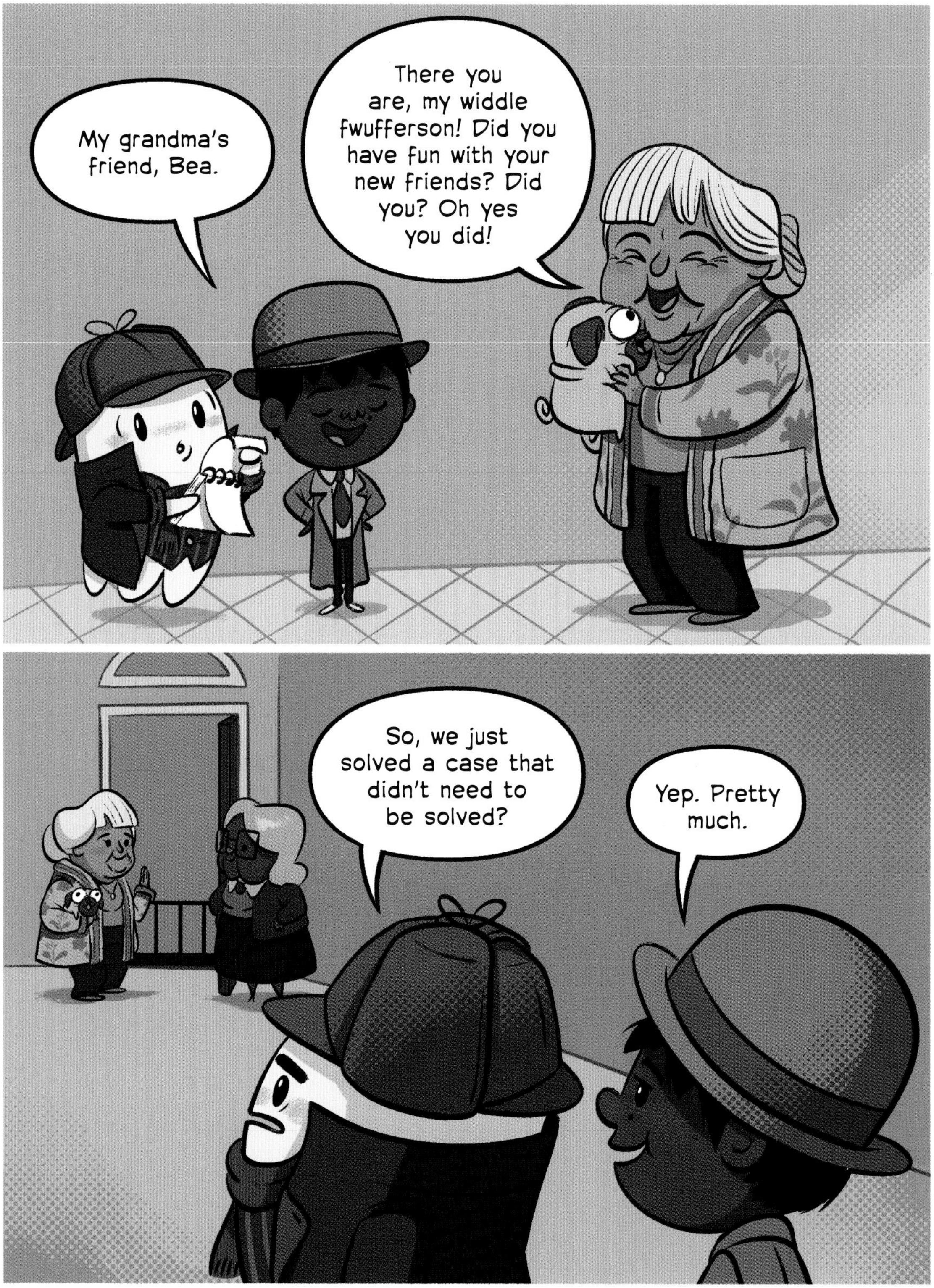
My grandma's friend, Bea.
There you are, my widdle fwufferson! Did you have fun with your new friends? Did you? Oh yes you did!
So, we just solved a case that didn't need to be solved?
Yep. Pretty much.

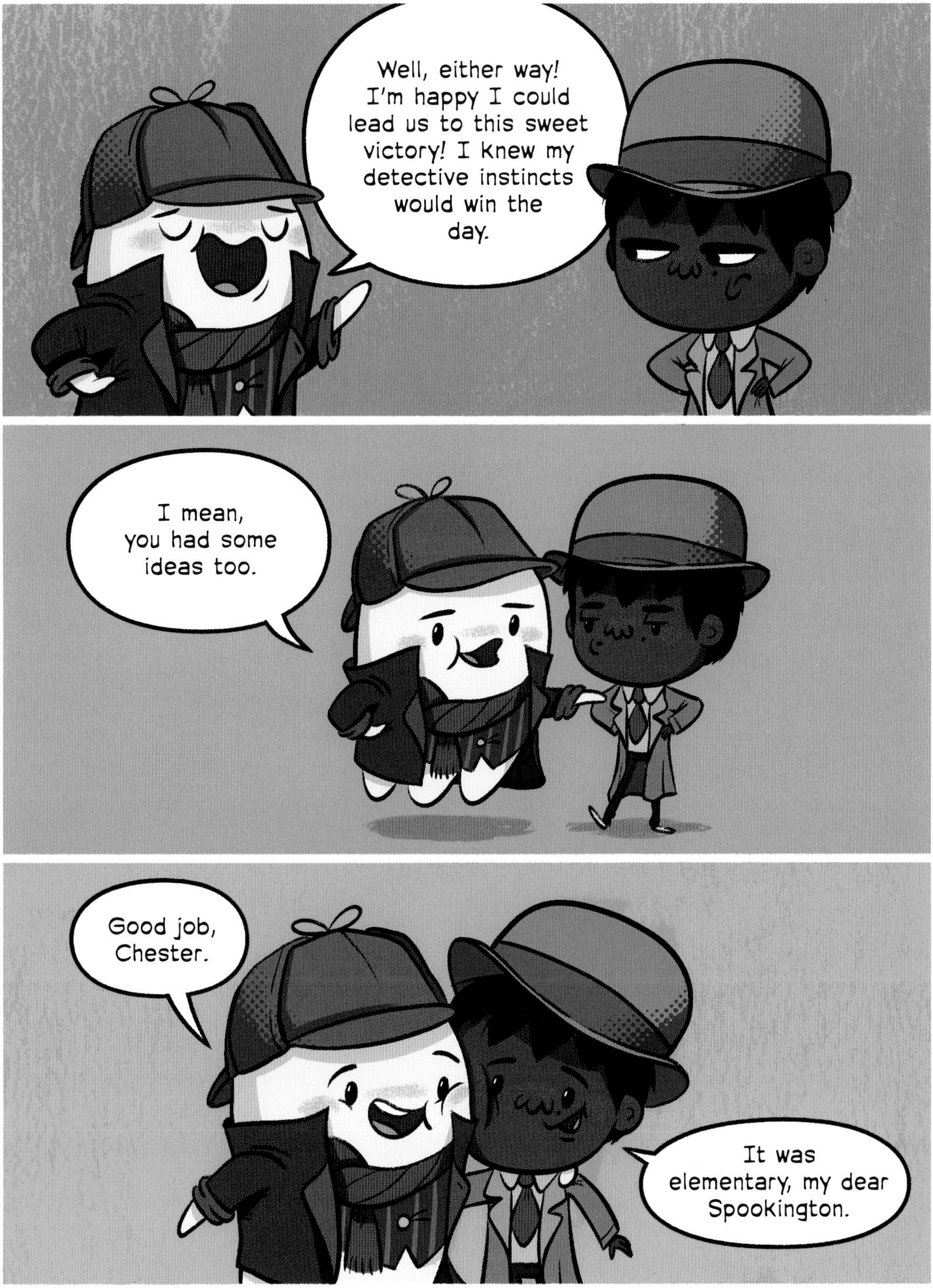
Well, either way! I'm happy I could lead us to this sweet victory! I knew my detective instincts would win the day.
I mean, you had some ideas too.
Good job, Chester.
It was elementary, my dear Spookington.

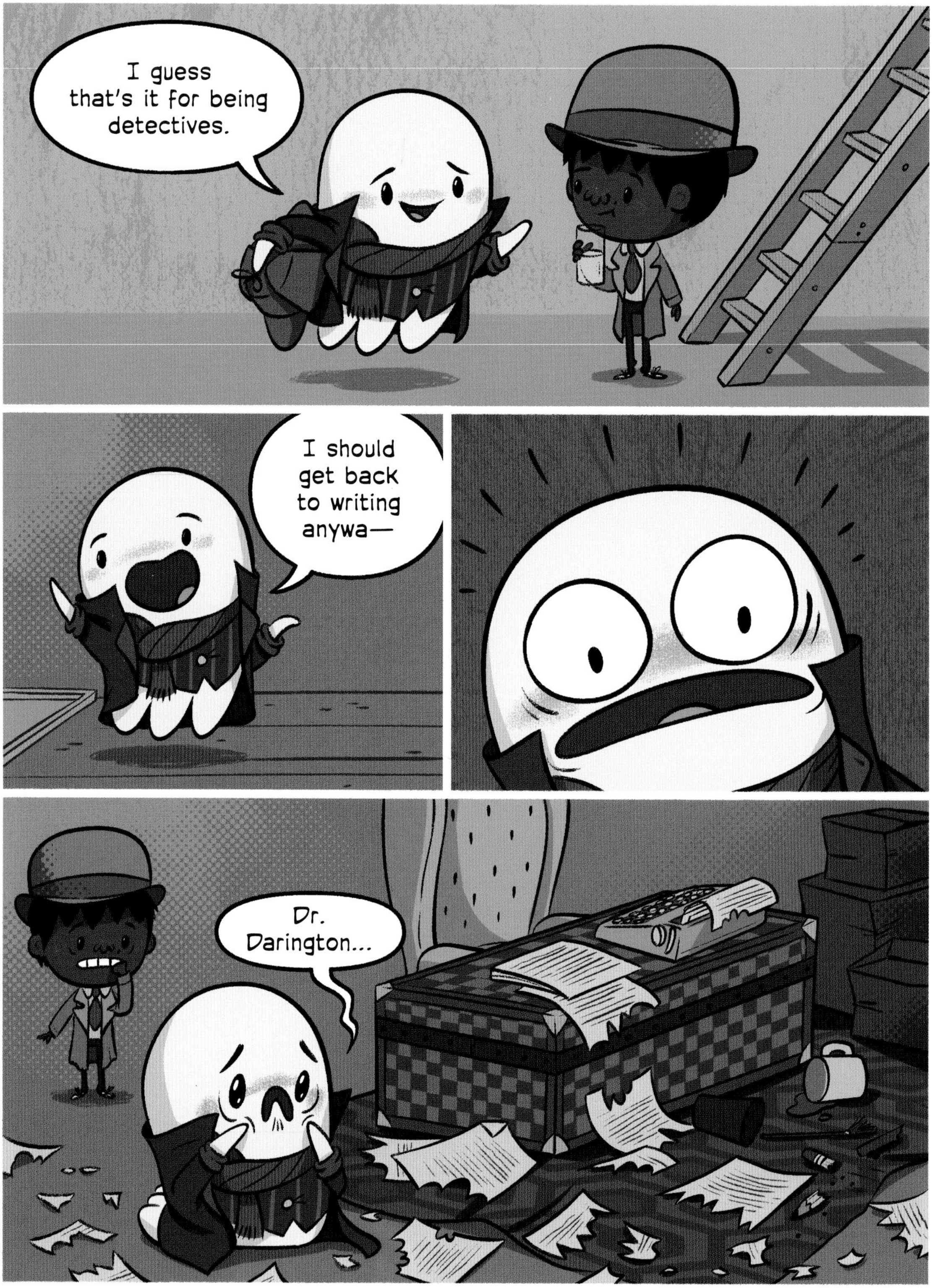
I guess that's it for being detectives.
I should get back to writing anywa—
Dr. Darington...

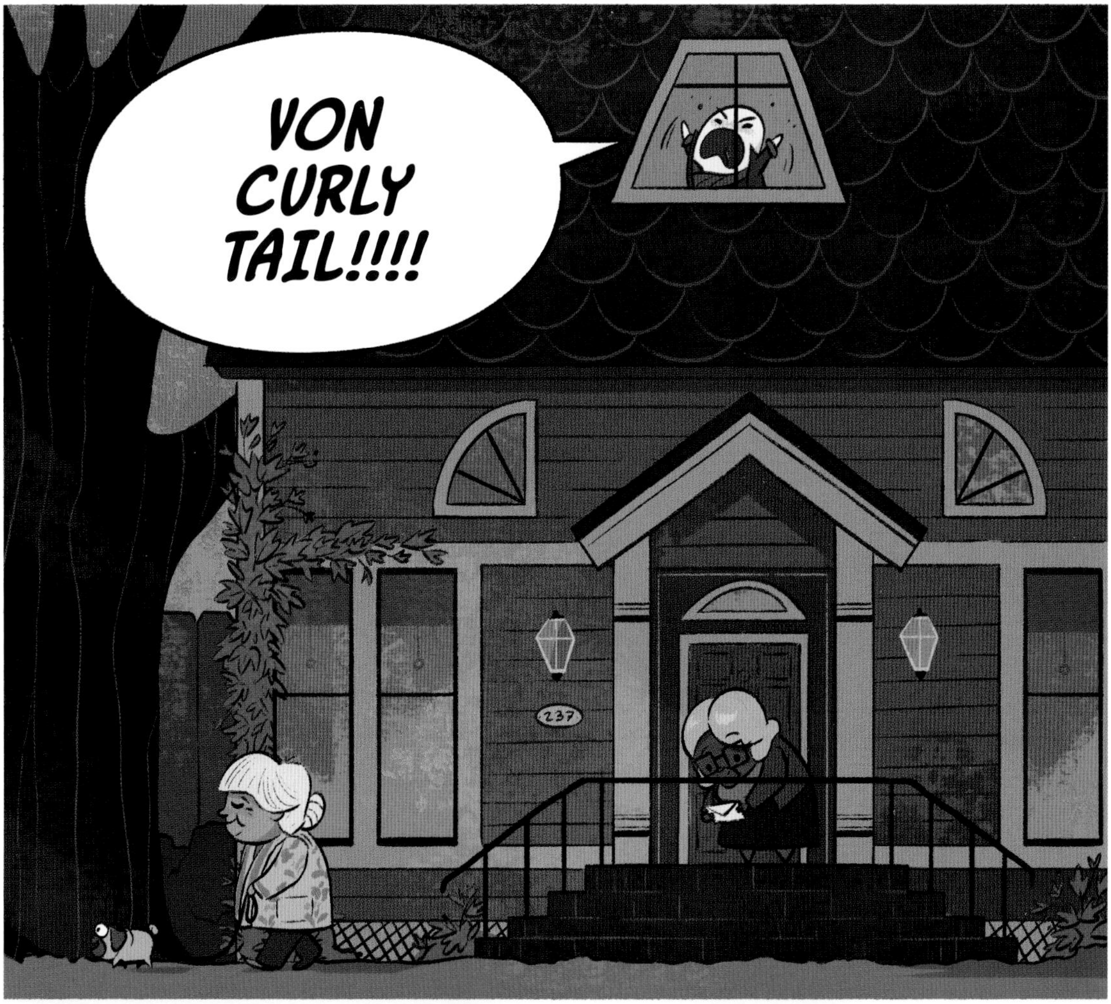
VON CURLY TAIL!!!!
237

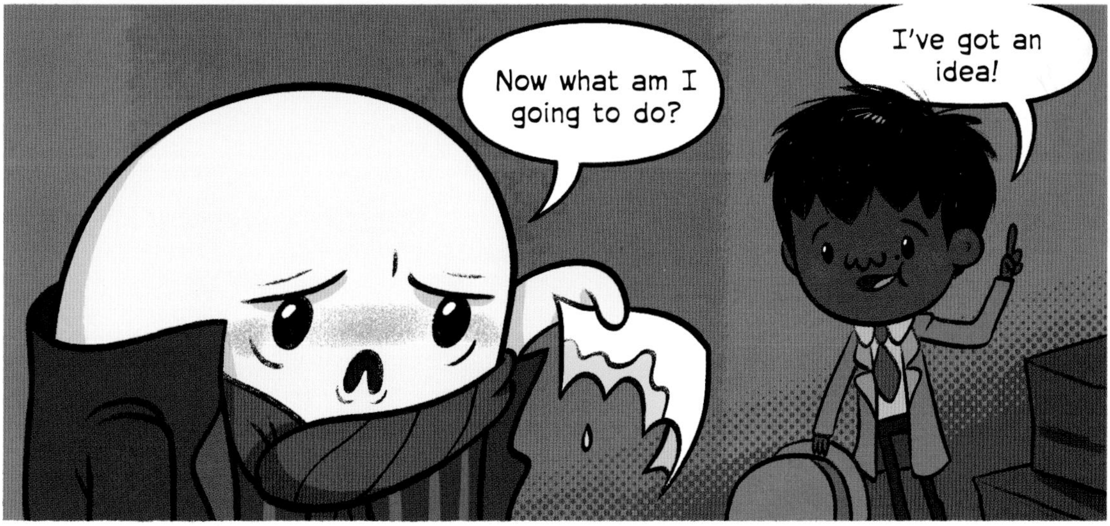
Now what am I going to do?
I've got an idea!

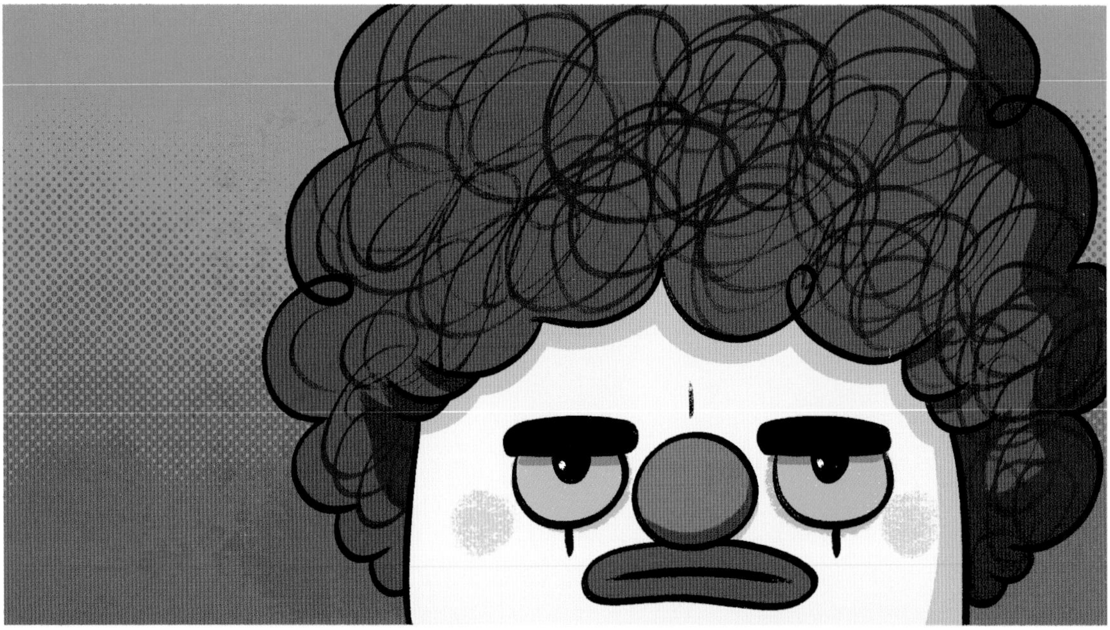

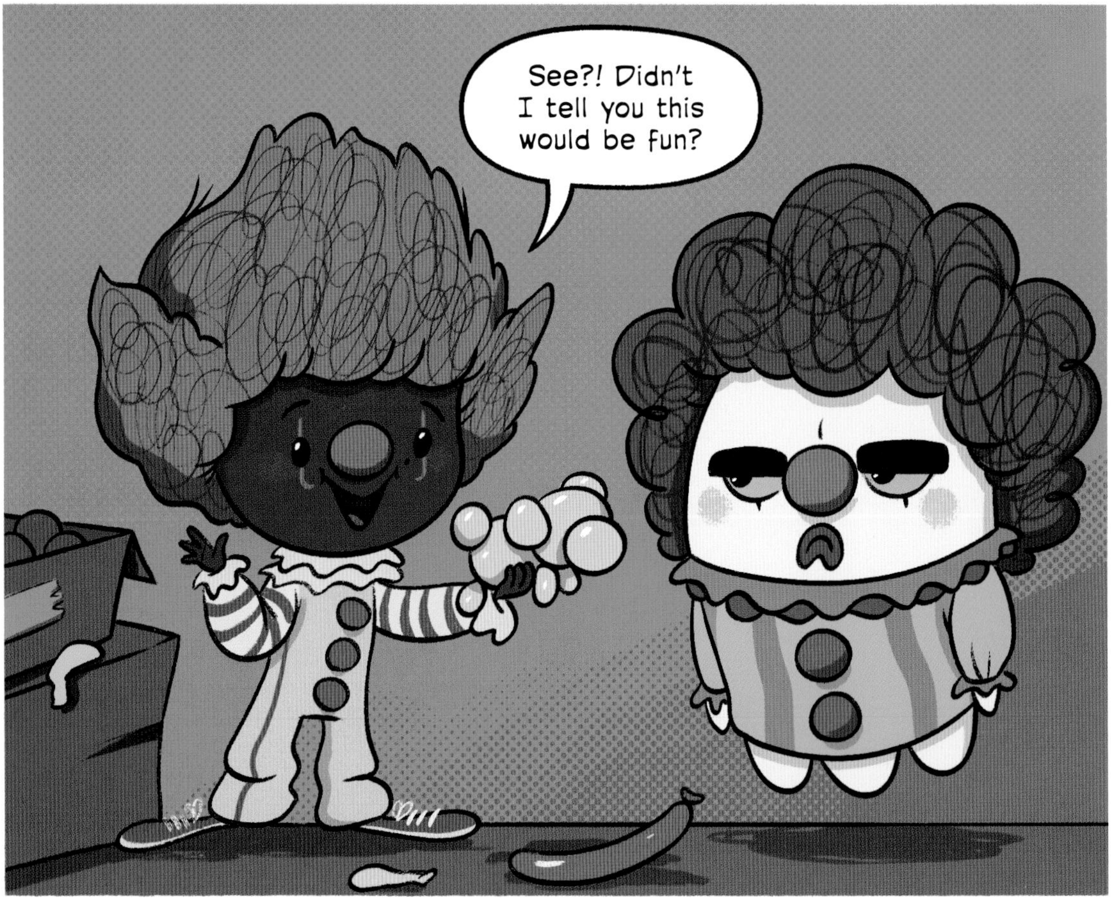
See?! Didn't I tell you this would be fun?